METROPOLITAN

BURGHS AND   SOUTHERN

PLAN of LONDON

drawn and engraved by: J.B. LANAHAN

& EASTERN ENVIRONS

METROPOLITAN BURGHS SOUTHERN & EASTERN ENVIRONS

READ

THE GLOBE

THE TRUTHFUL VOICE OF LONDON

established in 1803   established in 1803

Sherlock, Lupin & Me is published by Capstone Young Readers
A Capstone Imprint
1710 Roe Crest Drive
North Mankato, Minnesota 56003
www.capstoneyoungreaders.com

© 2012 Atlantyca Dreamfarm s.r.l., Italy
© 2015 for this book in English language - (Stone Arch Books/Capstone Young Readers)
Text by Pierdomenico Baccalario and Alessandro Gatti
Editorial project by Atlantyca Dreamfarm S.r.l., Italy
Translated into the English language by Nanette McGuinness
Original edition published by Edizioni Piemme S.p.A., Italy
Original title: Ultimo atto al teatro dell'Opera

Library of Congress Cataloging-in-Publication Data
Adler, Irene (Fictitious character), author.
 [Mistero della rosa scarlatta. English]

The mystery of the scarlet rose / by Irene Adler ; text by Pierdomenico Baccalario and Alessandro Gatti ; translated by Nanette McGuinness.

    pages cm. -- (Sherlock, Lupin, and me)

Summary: In London, at Christmas time in 1870, a strange message in the classified ads leads the three young detectives to murders that appear to be connected with the Scarlet Rose Gang, whose leader was killed years before.

ISBN 978-1-4342-6524-1 (library binding)
ISBN 978-1-62370-203-8 (paper over board)
ISBN 978-1-4342-6527-2 (pbk.)

1. Adler, Irene (Fictitious character)--Juvenile fiction. 2. Holmes, Sherlock--Juvenile fiction. 3. Lupin, Arsène (Fictitious character)--Juvenile fiction. 4. Murder--Investigation--England--Juvenile fiction. 5. Revenge--Juvenile fiction. 6. Detective and mystery stories. 7. London (England)--History--19th century--Juvenile fiction. [1. Mystery and detective stories. 2. Characters in literature--Fiction. 3. Murder--Fiction. 4. Revenge--Fiction. 5. London (England)--History--19th century--Fiction. 6. Great Britain--History--Victoria, 1837-1901--Fiction.] I. Baccalario, Pierdomenico, author. II. Gatti, Alessandro, author. III. McGuinness, Nanette, translator. IV. Title. V. Series: Adler, Irene (Fictitious character). Sherlock, Lupin & me.

 PZ7.A261545My 2015
 [Fic]--dc23
 2014024441

Designer: Veronica Scott

Printed in China.
092014   008472RRDS15

IRENE ADLER

SHERLOCK, LUPIN & ME

THE MYSTERY OF THE SCARLET ROSE

by Irene Adler
Illustrations by Jacopo Bruno

capstone
young readers

TABLE OF CONTENTS

Chapter 1

A LONDON CHRISTMAS

When I think back to that distant afternoon in December 1870, a clear image comes to mind: the slow dance of tiny snowflakes outside the window of Papa's study. It was my first London snowfall. Papa had gone to Glasgow for one of his business trips. With his typical generosity, he had agreed to let me do my schoolwork in his small, cozy study with book-lined walls.

Not far from me, a lively fire crackled in a small white marble fireplace. Horatio Nelson, our butler, walked toward the door he had left ajar and gestured to the window with a slight nod of his head. "Look, Miss Irene," he said.

As soon as I turned, the sight of all that whiteness surprised me, making my heart beat fast. "Snow! Snow!" I cried, without even thinking about it. I must have sounded like a little girl (or perhaps it would be more accurate to speak of the little girl who still lived inside me then).

Shortly thereafter, my mother arrived, having heard my outburst. Mr. Nelson stepped aside with a bow. I saw my mother look toward the window, her face lit up by a simple smile. She, too, after all, had the heart of a little girl.

"Oh, Irene . . . isn't it absolutely beautiful?" she asked.

"As lovely as a fairy tale," I answered.

My mother glanced at the books and papers cluttering Papa's desk and said, "I'll let you study, my dear. Until later."

I smiled, thinking that her good mood had a hidden meaning. After an autumn of sighs, long faces, and melancholy news from Paris (our home, which we'd had to flee suddenly due to the war with Prussia), perhaps London had finally won her over.

The elegance of the city buildings, the proper manners of good Londoners, and the stylish craftsmanship of the items sold in the luxury emporium — with which my mother had furnished our Aldford Street apartment — had, day after day, found their way into her heart. And when we heard from Papa's friends that many other women of Parisian society had also moved to the British capital to escape the dangers of the war, my mother's change was complete.

She no longer felt alone. Nor did I.

The Christmas atmosphere was enough to help us feel at home in this foreign city. And so those days that I spent with my mother were happy ones, as seldom had happened before.

This doesn't mean that I kept no secrets from her. On the contrary.

Even that afternoon, for example, I had not really been studying as she'd thought. Instead, I had just finished writing a page in the diary I'd begun several months before. A secret diary . . . a beautiful volume covered in Moroccan leather in which I disclosed many of the words that help me recall my childhood memories now. But I don't need to consult its now-yellowed pages to remember what I wrote that particular afternoon.

I wrote about my two dear friends, Sherlock Holmes and Arsène Lupin. The latter was traveling with his father and the Aronofsky Circus. His last postcard was dated from a month before and had been sent from Antwerp. When it arrived, Mr. Nelson secretly passed it to me and I read it in my room, my stomach fluttering with excitement.

Remembering that last letter, I sighed and kept my eyes glued to the delicate dance of snowflakes outside the window.

Sherlock Holmes, on the other hand, had become a frequent visitor since I'd moved to the capital of Britain. I knew I was a lucky girl now that I lived in London — and not just because my father was able to get us away from the violence of the Franco-Prussian War. But I was also lucky because even before fame had brushed my friend, I realized what a privilege it was to spend time with Sherlock Holmes and witness his lively, volatile genius.

However, there were times I missed Lupin, with his charming simplicity and his boldness. I missed his ability to make even the most dangerous adventure seem harmless but then describe it in such an exaggerated way that I had a hard time recognizing it, despite having been involved myself. I missed Lupin's jokes, his confidence, his bold daredevil actions, and that feeling of invincibility he seemed to have in the face of the world around us, which reassured me before all danger.

Mostly, I missed the alchemy that was created when the three of us — Sherlock, Lupin, and I — were together.

That was the power of our youth and our friendship.

Yes, I was lucky to have such dear friends. And lucky to have had so many adventures with them. It was hard to believe that just last summer, we'd been carrying out our first investigation. After we'd come across a dead body washed ashore on the beach in Saint-Malo, the three of us had vowed to discover the man's identity and the cause of his death. Indeed, we did discover those facts . . . and then some.

Just a few short months after, I visited London with Papa. It was then that Sherlock, Lupin, and I began a different investigation, this one into the murder of Alfred Santi, assistant to the great opera maestro, Guiseppe Barzini. This investigation had hit a rather personal note since Lupin's father, Théophraste, was accused of the murder. When the famous opera singer, Ophelia Merridew, went missing, our trio had set out to find her. And we'd been successful.

I sighed, wondering what adventure we might encounter next.

When I finally tore my eyes away from the window, I hurried to check the clock in the corner of the office. It was Wednesday, a few minutes before three. And that day of the week, as well as on Fridays, my afternoons were spent the same way — at four o'clock on the dot, I would go down to the street, where Mr. Nelson waited with a carriage to take me to the Shackleton Coffee House on Carnaby Street.

That was one of the little secrets I shared with our butler. My parents believed I was going to my lesson with Miss Langtry, my new voice teacher. The truth, however, was that I went there an hour later, after spending some time with Sherlock in the Shackleton Coffee House, a café that was little suited for a young girl from a good family. But because Mr. Nelson was responsible for scheduling and paying

Miss Langtry, it was not difficult to tell that small lie and gain that short, secret moment in the company of my fascinating friend, the young Sherlock Holmes.

That day, however, the unexpected snowfall convinced me to change my routine. I hurried to put Papa's desk back in order and ran to my bedroom to put on my heaviest boots. Then I bundled up, announcing my plans to Mr. Nelson and my mother as I was already heading out the door.

"I'm going to walk to Miss Langtry today! I want to enjoy the city in the snow! Could you send the usual carriage to fetch me at six, Mr. Nelson?" I asked.

While my mother's and Mr. Nelson's voices echoed from the front hall behind me, I plunged outside into the cold air and the swirls of snow that had slipped between the buildings, carriages, and bundled-up passersby.

I intended to go meet Sherlock, of course, but I hadn't been lying when I'd said I wanted to enjoy the city in the snow. So I crossed Aldford Street and turned onto South Adley Street, heading toward Piccadilly. It wasn't the shortest route, but as I came out to the large, bustling street that led to the heart of London, I found all that I had hoped to find.

First of all, the majestic trees of Green Park were now covered in snow, and their branches intertwined like silver lattices. I found myself thinking about something that had struck me years before, when I was a child — the incredible wizardry that snow can create. It can transform even the most forgettable corner of a city into a magical place, enchanted and mysterious.

I gazed at the lights beaming inside the grand hotels and the glowing shop windows and the comings and goings of ladies dressed in fur, their valets huffing and puffing under bags and suitcases. In that moment, I felt that special, feverish merriment that can only come when walking down a city street in the days before Christmas.

I found myself surrounded by voices, laughter, and the aroma of roasted chestnuts and sugar loaves, and happily let myself be swept up in the rushing stream of people. I enjoyed every single moment of that walk in the snow, captivated by the bright colors, the decorations, and the mistletoe branches in the shop windows. It all looked like a giant kaleidoscope.

Almost without realizing it, I reached Piccadilly Circus, where — between the crowds of people and the traffic of carriages and wagons — it was nearly impossible to move. I turned onto the first road that led north and walked quickly for a quarter of an hour. I let the smell of roasting sausages and the cries of shopkeepers guide me through a neighborhood much simpler and more working-class than the one I'd just left. I arrived at Carnaby Street and wove my way between market stalls and the bustling crowd of people.

I finally walked through the doorway of the Shackleton Coffee House and, despite being twenty minutes early, found Sherlock already sunk into his favorite armchair. Seeing him filled me with the usual intense thrill, which felt like a slight tightening in my stomach.

But there was a black cloud that seemed to swirl around Sherlock's eternally disheveled hair. I sensed an air of unrest and gloom, which immediately put me on alert.

Indeed, I knew Sherlock Holmes too well not to recognize that something must have happened.

Chapter 2

A SUDDEN STORM

My intuition had hit the bull's-eye: Sherlock's greeting came in the form of a grunt.

"Good day to you, Holmes," I teased. "I'm glad to see that the sparkling Christmas atmosphere has made you cheerful."

Sherlock threw me one of his intense looks. His hard, gray eyes twinkled for a moment, and then he covered them with his hand, rubbing his face. In the middle of his forehead, which up to that point had been smooth and relaxed, two wrinkles formed, and his long, sharp nose twitched with annoyance.

"At the moment, my mind is an endless desert of boredom," he said. "And I am sorry to inform you that what you call the 'Christmas atmosphere' simply does not exist."

"Really?" I said as I sat down in an armchair across the table from Sherlock. "And yet it appears that I just saw a few thousand merry Londoners walking the streets, ready to contradict your odd theory . . . "

Sherlock responded with a sneer. "I do not understand why people are so merry!" he said, crossing his legs in an irritated fashion. Then he extended his long, knobby fingers one by one as he listed everything that seemed incomprehensible to him. "Streets blocked by foolish people, smiles engraved on their faces, greedy shopkeepers eager to sell useless rubbish, and a pathetic race to eat greasy food . . . is that your idea of a 'sparkling' atmosphere?" grumbled my friend.

"I think you should send a formal petition to abolish Christmas to Her Majesty Queen Victoria," I said. "Then you'll have taken care of the problem."

Sherlock grasped his cup of hot cocoa, took a sip, and grunted again. Then he smiled, and I did the same.

By then, I knew those moments of dark humor very well. And Sherlock knew that I was certainly not going to be crushed by the grip of his anger. What he would never admit, however, not even under torture, was that my presence helped calm him. And that he'd wanted to meet me at least as much as I'd wanted to meet him.

"The truth," he admitted, after ordering a cup of hot cocoa for me, "is that I am now decidedly less irritated than I was just half an hour ago, Irene."

"I've always had a certain influence on you," I kidded, putting my gloves on the small table. But the truth is, I liked to imagine that what I'd just said was really so. "And if I might ask," I continued, "to what do we owe this lucky improvement in your mood?"

"It's because of the good old *Times!*" Sherlock answered, grabbing a copy of the paper that was lying on the windowsill next to him.

I felt a stab of disappointment, which I ignored.

"Oh. It seems there would be reading material that might serve your mood better than the *Times*," I answered, surprised.

"And you are right," admitted Sherlock, flipping through the pages. "But this page of classified ads in Monday's *Times* contains an interesting . . . peculiarity."

"If you're referring to that blurb about the little Indian monkeys trained to steal wallets out of the pockets of well-meaning people, well . . . Mr. Nelson already spoke to me about that at length. Even he was struck by it," I said.

"Not the little monkeys. It's this," answered Sherlock, pointing to a small box in the corner of the page.

I leaned over to read an ad entitled "Chess Problem." It had three rows of letters and numbers, starting with, "V2 – P19 – Q2," followed by the phrase, "Checkmate in three moves," and ending with the signature, "The Black Friar."

"Sorry," I said, leaning back in the armchair. It was typical of Sherlock to pore over the paper to find the tiniest details. He always read the small announcements and ads more carefully than the front-page news. "The game of chess is not really a strength of mine. Is it a stimulating problem?"

"That's exactly what's curious," answered my friend. "Whatever this thing is, it's definitely not a chess problem."

"Excuse me, but how can you be so sure?" I asked.

Sherlock snorted and leaned across the table. "It's simple! It so happens that a while ago, in an attempt to survive a boring, endless summer —"

"I hope it wasn't the one when we met each other," I interrupted him, teasing.

"One much worse, I can guarantee you," Sherlock said. He paused, and I thought perhaps he, too, was thinking back to when we saw each other for the first time on the ramparts of Saint-Malo. He'd been hopelessly lost in the pages of a book, looking for an intellectual challenge that could keep him from being crushed by the muggy weather and all the history that surrounded us.

No, last summer had been anything other than boring, I thought, and I got ready to hear the rest of the story.

"At that time," he continued, "I became a fan of chess. I read a good deal and learned all the systems of chess notation that I could get my hands on, trying to repeat the great games of the masters of the past."

"Chess notation?" I repeated. "What exactly does that consist of? It's Greek to me."

"It's simple," he said. "Chess notation is how you represent the position of the pieces on the chessboard at a given moment in the game by using sequences of letters, numbers, and other symbols."

"A type of code, in other words," I said.

"Precisely! And I can assure you, this thing the peculiar Black Friar published is not written in any existing chess notation."

"Perhaps he's just an oddball who uses his own code," I suggested.

"For what reason?" Sherlock replied. "What would the purpose be of getting a chess problem published in the paper that no one, except the writer, could understand?"

"Boredom?" I suggested.

Sherlock ignored me and continued speaking. "Not to mention there's no way to guess at this sequence! No way to understand what the position of the pieces on the chessboard could be! I've been racking my brain for almost an hour without getting anywhere."

Almost an hour of concentrating for an obsessive mind like Sherlock's was truly an eternity!

I glimpsed that unmistakable twinkle in his eye that conveyed his need to share what was going on in his head with me. At my nod, Sherlock launched into an explanation of why the classified ad could not simply be a chess problem.

I confess that I quickly gave up on following his long, complicated lecture, of which I only grasped parts, hoping that would be enough to paint a clearer picture of the situation for me.

Algebraic notation.

Smith method.

Gringmuth system.

Sherlock, interpreting my silence as a sign of agreement, pulled a small, dark notebook and a pencil from his pocket, intending to convince me beyond any doubt that his conclusion was correct.

"I've no intention of taking a course in such a tedious subject, Professor Holmes!" I interrupted. "It's enough for me to see that vein on your forehead to know it's just as you say."

He stared at me, bewildered, and brought his hand to his temple, where the bluish vein in question pulsed energetically.

Never underestimate a girl's powers of observation, I thought, smiling. Then I added, "The only point I don't understand is what could be so exciting about all this."

"It seems elementary to me," answered Sherlock, putting the notebook and pencil back in his pocket, an astonished look on his face. "The inevitable question we must ask is this: if the Black Friar's classified listing isn't a chess problem, then what the devil is it? And," he continued before I could chime in, "why hide it in the pages of the newspaper? I'm afraid these questions will keep me from sleeping tonight."

I laughed.

It was true. A tiny unsolved mystery like this was, for Sherlock Holmes, capable of ruining a night's sleep. I was about to ask him how he intended to proceed solving the mystery, and if I could help him in any way, when the door to the Shackleton Coffee House burst open.

A striking figure appeared in the doorway in a gust of wind and snow. He was wrapped up in an elegant crimson coat, with a gray felt cap pulled down over his face.

"I'll be darned!" Sherlock immediately exclaimed, sitting up against the back of his armchair.

A second look at the café entrance was all it took for me to be as flabbergasted as he was.

The patron who'd just entered the café had taken off his hat and scarf, and his face was now clearly recognizable.

It was Arsène Lupin!

Chapter 3

A SOUL IN TURMOIL

"I knew I'd find you here!" crowed our French friend, throwing his coat onto the nearest chair. He looked at both of us and, after a moment's hesitation, hugged me first, gently squeezing me. We lightly kissed each other's cheeks like old friends. Then Lupin threw his arms around Sherlock. Their hug was more spontaneous, with wild pats on the back and a couple of rough handshakes. I looked at them, smiling, with a touch of envy.

In the few months he'd been away, Lupin seemed to have grown a good deal more than Sherlock or I had. Despite the winter season, he was tan, his eyes were dark and shining, and his cheekbones and jaw were carved as if by a sculptor. He had a healthy, agile physique, with the poise of someone who leads an active life. His movements were never accidental or clumsy. Looking at him strike a pose in that foreign café with absolute ease was like watching a hot knife slip through a stick of butter.

To tell the truth, that morning I disliked watching my two friends from the outside, separate, instead of being completely involved in the three of us reuniting.

I mean, I was very happy but also so excited that I retreated inside myself a little, to protect myself from the effect that my two friends had on me.

We all started speaking together, without even taking the time to sit down, and so, when a confused waiter came by to ask Lupin for his order, we burst out laughing and finally sat down around the table.

"Now, then!" Lupin smiled at me, putting his hand on mine, which he stroked with affection. "What's been happening with you all this time? Have I missed anything?"

I felt my fingers tremble under his. I looked at

Sherlock, because Lupin had asked both of us what had been going on.

I gave a brief answer and then asked in turn, "But what are you doing here, all of a sudden, and without letting anyone know?"

"Bof!" exclaimed my young friend. "Do you want the truth?"

"As much as possible," answered Sherlock. "As much as you can tell."

Lupin lifted his hand from mine with a final stroke, and I quickly put mine back in my lap, like a wounded little bird. I listened to the story that followed, confused.

Arsène had had a fierce argument with his father, Théophraste, and had decided to leave the circus.

"You mean you came to London . . . alone?" I asked him, astonished.

He chuckled, halfway between being amused and offended, as if I should have seen a grown man in him and not a boy a few years older than me.

"*Bien sûr!*" he answered. "And it was the best decision of my life."

He told us that his father's traveling circus had stopped in Rotterdam not long before, where a rich city merchant had made fun of Théophraste's acrobatic number.

"Such an ignoramus, my friends! I couldn't stand it," Lupin confided to us, flashing that ferret-like smirk that made me happy.

"So what did you do?" Sherlock asked him.

"I challenged him to a game of cards," Lupin replied, "that very evening. And, of course . . . I cleaned him out of everything he had — even his watch."

My eyes widened. "Cleaned him out?"

He closed his fingers and then opened them as swiftly as a falcon. Between his index finger and thumb, he held the ace of diamonds. "Cleaned him out with great skill and sleight of hand!" he said.

"Magnificent!" Sherlock exclaimed, slapping his hand on the table. "Now you're talking!"

I was not so easily convinced, however. "You cheated at cards for money?" I asked.

"For the family honor," Lupin specified, my question not shaking his self-confidence in the least.

"Quite right," said Sherlock, who seemed more interested in how Lupin had made a card appear in his hand than in the rest of the affair.

"But it wasn't your money!" I blurted out.

"That's what my father said," Arsène replied, stung. He looked at us in search of agreement. "He scolded me the whole evening, ordering me to return the money. You should have heard him. He lectured me — tried to take the moral high ground with me! After all the work we had to do to get him out of prison! And after everything he did when he was young!"

Exactly, I thought. "Perhaps that's why he didn't want you to —" I began, but I was interrupted by a second enthusiastic outburst from Sherlock Holmes.

"A drink for my friend!" he cried to the waiter, abandoning all traces of British poise. "And for us, too!"

At the time I didn't know, except for a tiny intuition I had, that Sherlock had a personal reason for agreeing with Arsène, for admiring his friend's decision to leave his family.

Upon the death of his father eight years earlier, Sherlock, the middle child, had shouldered many of the family responsibilities. He cared for his littlest sister, making up for the excesses of his older brother Mycroft. Sherlock's mother had decided to invest their few financial resources in Mycroft, allowing him to attend the best schools. As a result, Mycroft became a successful politician in London society some fifteen years later. But he never was an immortal character like Sherlock Holmes, who studied his brother's schoolbooks on his own, without any recognition.

This, then, explained the reason Sherlock understood immoral acts like cheating, stealing money, and disobeying one's father, which only seemed like childish choices and bad taste to me.

I did not yet know what inner turmoil could be unleashed in a child's heart upon discovering the truth about one's own family and real parents. What I mean is, I already knew with some certainty that my mother and my dear papa were not my real parents. But I didn't have the least idea who my real parents were . . . nor of how profoundly this knowledge would change the course of my life.

"I heard that there's going to be an exhibit in Paddington of the latest technological wonders in the world," Lupin said at that point. "What do you say we go on Friday? It's on me!"

I was deeply disturbed about how Lupin seemed to be enjoying his freedom, and when I saw him shelling out the wad of banknotes he'd won from the merchant, I showed every bit of my disapproval and stood up abruptly.

"What's wrong?" Sherlock asked. Only then did my two friends realize how distant I was acting toward them.

"Nothing," I lied. "I just promised my mother something."

"So what?" Lupin said. "Tell her you changed your mind and that you're going with us to the fair!"

I put on my gloves, annoyed. "I'm afraid that's simply not possible, Arsène. That's not how it's done."

Still seated with the banknotes in his hands, he blinked a couple of times. "*Pardon?*" he asked.

Just then, Sherlock got up. "Arsène is right," he said to me. "It's a lovely idea. Let's all three of us go."

"Do you think so, Sherlock?" I asked him, in a more snobbish tone than I'd really wanted to use.

"Rebel before it's too late!" Lupin exclaimed. "Make the most of your time!"

"It's not what you think," I lied. "My mother and I need to do something very important!"

"You're wrong," Lupin said. "Those are just

promises. And you have to toss them behind you like my friend Hilda did."

"Hilda?" I repeated.

"Yes, Hilda!" said Lupin. And looking at Sherlock, he explained. "She's a girl from a good family who I met in Hamburg. Believe me, she's very, very pretty. And she ran away from home to join our circus!"

It was too much.

I turned on my heel and walked out of the Shackleton Coffee House.

Let those two talk about that Hilda and pretty girls, if they wanted. But they would do it alone.

★ ★ ★

My singing lesson was a complete disaster, and when Mr. Nelson came to pick me up in the carriage at six, he asked me what had happened.

"Did you have a fight with your friend, Miss Irene?" he asked me in an understanding tone.

"Absolutely not," I answered.

And that was all I felt like saying. The truth was that my heart was confused, and that night I had difficulty falling asleep.

The promise I'd made to my mother was to sew

little rag dolls that would be sold to benefit the city's poor children. And when I began to work on them a while later, I threw myself into it with the ironclad conviction that it was the right thing to do. I thought that with the help of those dolls, I would stop thinking about Sherlock and Lupin. Especially Lupin. But it didn't work. It seemed my hands couldn't move. My mother talked to me the entire time, and I answered in monosyllables without remembering a single word she said.

I don't know what made me feel worse: having judged Lupin over cheating at cards, feeling judged myself by my friends, or more simply, jealousy of that Hilda. Who was she? Why had she joined the circus? And why had Lupin felt the need to say that she was very beautiful?

I felt ashamed by the idea of what Lupin might have ever said about me, ashamed of the kiss stolen when we were hidden in the room of the Hotel Albion, and ashamed of the fact that I was wondering whether he considered Hilda to be more or less pretty than I was.

I spent an entire dinner looking at myself in my mirror, instead of at the table eating with my mother, trying to decide whether or not I was very beautiful, too. I had a small nose and a delicate chin, yes, but maybe my eyes were too round. And my mouth, except in profile, seemed out of proportion, with lips that were too large. And too toothy! And my earlobes? Were they too close to my neck? My neck was very long . . . funny-looking probably. And I wasn't sure if my bodice should draw so much attention to the shape of my figure. I was very tall, certainly, and this seemed nice. But I was a girl . . . perhaps a beautiful girl shouldn't be tall. Or maybe it was that beauty mark that my friend didn't like.

But how was I really so sure that Arsène didn't like me? And did it really matter so much to me?

I rearranged my long red hair from one side of my face to the other, gathered it uselessly into braids and then a bun. I finally stopped, as full of doubt as I'd ever been.

A few minutes later, I found myself in my bed, sleepless but exhausted. I tossed hopelessly from side to side. Everything looked white to me, although it actually was dark. All of London was resting serenely outside my window. The only sound that reached me from time to time was the tolling of the bell from . . .

I turned over again, trying not to rack my brain to figure out which belltower it belonged to. I sank my face against my pillow, grumbling into it. My nightgown was soaked with sweat.

"Stop it!" I cried out, when the persistent tolling became unbearable. How many times did that bell have to sound in the dead of the night?

As if to satisfy me, the tolling suddenly stopped. I turned on the lamp on my nightstand, thinking that if I wasn't going to sleep, I could at least read something. *But not Flaubert,* I thought. *Let other people read his detailed descriptions of romantic sentiments.* I only wanted to read about mysteries, adventures, and terrifying locations. Where were Mary Shelley, Sheridan Le Fanu, and that American, Edgar Allan Poe, whose stories Mr. Nelson loved?

I placed one foot on the floor and took a step, which made the floor creak. Then the bells started up again.

A shiver ran down my sweaty back, and my brain suddenly fogged up. It wasn't a distant bell, but something close to me. A series of rhythmic blows against the wooden shutters, as if . . . something, or someone . . .

Struck by a strange idea, I crossed the room and cracked the window open. A voice from outside called to me, "Irene?"

I brought my hand to my throat, afraid. But then, without even thinking about it, I finished opening the window and shutters. I had barely done so when I found myself face to face with Sherlock and Lupin, who were clinging to the gutter.

"What are you two doing here?" I asked, stunned.

"May we speak with you . . . a little more comfortably?" begged Sherlock. The effort of hanging there had clearly begun to take its toll on him.

I doubt that the family rules I had so energetically upheld at the café would have included allowing two young daredevils such as Sherlock and Lupin to sneak into my bedroom and receive them, whispering, in my nightgown.

But I didn't hesitate to do so.

I sat on my bed while they perched on the two uncomfortable seats across from me in the shadows.

I tucked my nightgown under my knees and asked, "So? Are you crazed . . . or what?"

The two looked at each other, as if to decide who should start explaining. It fell to Lupin.

"Listen, Irene . . . the thing is . . . " He paused and sighed. "Sherlock and I want to apologize."

"Ah," I said. "What for?"

"You know very well," Lupin said.

He was right, of course, but I still waited for him to continue.

"I'm very sorry," he went on. "I . . . we are very sorry. Today in the café I behaved like a real fool."

"And I with him," said Sherlock. He kept his eyes down, ashamed.

"We didn't mean to offend you," Lupin continued. "Especially . . ."

He stopped. A noise from the hallway seemed to have worried him.

"Especially?" I asked.

"Especially, we didn't want you to leave," Lupin continued. "I came to the Shackleton Coffee House just because . . . it was the one place where I knew . . . I thought . . . I hoped . . . I would find my friends."

As he spoke, my blood felt warm as it coursed through my veins. But I stayed silent and listened, not wanting to admit it.

"My only two friends. One and the other," Lupin said.

"Arsène and I wanted you to know that nothing has changed since those days in Saint-Malo," Sherlock added. "From the friendship we formed there."

"That's right," Lupin confirmed. He nodded slowly.

Since it seemed as if he didn't have anything else to tell me, I whispered, "I'm glad."

"And to prove this to you," Lupin exclaimed suddenly, "Holmes has some sensational news to tell you."

"Really, Holmes?" I asked, turning toward him.

"Quite so," he answered, pulling three small books out of his jacket as he walked toward my bed, ignoring the fact that we were immersed in deep shadows.

"Sherlock . . ." I tried to interrupt him, but he was absorbed in thought, opening the three volumes and placing them on my bed.

"The fact is," he went on, "I finally solved the problem of the Black Friar. Do you remember it? Just as we thought, it wasn't a chess problem but a code."

I mentally thanked him for giving me partial credit for forming that hypothesis, given that he had really come up with it on his own.

Sherlock pointed a finger at the middle of one of the three books, making the second-rate paper it was printed on crackle. "The code didn't indicate the coordinates of a chessboard, but a specific place in London as it appears in *Furlong Street Guide,* the most accurate map of the city that exists."

"Oh," I said, far from captivated.

A strange silence fell. It was broken by the quivering voice of Lupin, who whispered, "Tell her, Sherlock."

Sherlock hesitated a little too long.

"Tell me what?" I asked, leaning forward so I could see his eyes.

"The amazing thing," he began, and I felt myself swallow a glob of saliva, "is that the code is across three lines, and every line indicates a place on the map of London."

"So in all there are . . . three different locations?" I asked.

"Exactly. And at the first one . . . " Sherlock said, lowering his finger on the map a little, "a horrible murder has just been committed."

Chapter 4

THREE CHILDREN AT SCOTLAND YARD

The next morning, I awoke very early. I kept flipping through the newspaper that Sherlock had left for me. It was a copy of the second evening edition of the *Standard*, one of the most widely read papers in London. It was the copy that Sherlock's brother Mycroft had brought when he'd come home, and it was the same copy that had made my friend jump from his chair as soon as his eyes fell on the short article.

It reported the murder of a certain Samuel Peccary, a rich fur merchant who was stabbed at his luxurious waterfront mansion in the suburb of Twickenham.

According to what Sherlock and Lupin had managed to explain in those few excited moments in my room that night, the "chess problem" consisted of three codes, each referring to an exact coordinate on a specific page in the *Furlong Street Guide*.

As soon as Sherlock had figured out the possible nature of the Black Friar's coded message, the two had rushed to the nearest bookstore to purchase the three volumes of the guide.

After a quick check, we found that Sherlock's hypothesis was completely possible. The three brief codes referred to the volume number, page, and finally, the coordinates in the *Furlong Street Guide*, and so they identified three locations in the city. The first of the three was in Twickenham on the Thames River, while the other two were closer to the city center.

As I got ready to eat breakfast, I did not find it hard to imagine Sherlock and Lupin seated in the café or in the tiny wooden toolshed in Holmes's backyard, intent on sorting out what was significant about these three corners of London. I could imagine the flash of light that must have gone through Sherlock's eyes when the news blurb in the *Standard* unexpectedly answered that question.

If the first spot was the scene of a homicide, then the next two might be places where murders have yet to occur!

This explained Sherlock and Lupin's nighttime visit, which had been a perfectly reckless idea considering what might have happened if my mother had discovered us.

Instead, I had never been so happy. The first thing my friends had done, as soon as they'd discovered the possibility of the crime, was come look for me. Knowing that made my heart overflow with joy. Those few moments spent whispering in the darkness of my room erased all the misunderstandings of our previous encounter.

I felt foolish. All it took for me to be poisoned by jealousy was hearing Lupin say the name of another girl. Did I really think that Lupin, traveling all over Europe with his father, would live the life of a recluse? The truth was, I was envious of his and Hilda's freedom. Hilda really was braver than I was, as her decisions proved.

But there was also another, sweeter truth. In that surprise nighttime visit, Sherlock, Lupin, and I were once again united in our special way, leaving the rest of the world behind. It had only taken a few moments of scheming to renew our bond and make it seem as if we had never been apart.

That was what I was thinking about during the two hours I had to spend with Mrs. Symonds, my new instructor for Latin and English Literature lessons. They were absolute torture, and it seemed to me as though time had unkindly halted right in the middle of them. But the lessons finally ended, and I was once again free to go.

As usual, I needed a little white lie and Mr. Nelson's help. He was to tell my mother we had gone to Portobello Road to look for Christmas presents. Instead, he would go alone while I met up with my friends.

"Shall I choose your gifts, Miss Irene?" asked the butler, whom I now considered a faithful friend. Mr. Nelson smiled mysteriously and aimed his dark, intense eyes at me.

"Why do I have the impression that your eyes are trying to tell me something?" I asked.

"My eyes have just noticed you expressing a certain . . . energy. The kind of energy you have when certain friends are in town," answered the butler.

How Mr. Nelson had known Lupin was in town was a mystery to me, at least until — when sitting in the carriage taking me to 55 Cheapside — I remembered the little noise we had heard from inside the apartment the previous evening. That noise could well have been Horatio Nelson, stopping to eavesdrop outside my bedroom door.

My carriage arrived in front of St. Paul's School, where Sherlock had begun attending a couple months before, and I paid the coachman for the ride. Just then, I saw Lupin arrive in a carriage on the opposite side of the street.

I raced across the busy street.

"Hello, Irene!" Lupin greeted me, grinning.

"It's a pleasure to see you again in daylight. I, however, prefer you in the dark," I teased. Lupin looked handsome and elegant, even though he was dressed in the same wrinkled clothes from the day before. I took a seat next to him in the carriage, and we waited.

Lupin looked up at the grand school building. "It would seem our schoolboy hasn't yet managed to escape the clutches of his schoolmaster!" he said.

In fact, due to a trick of fate, the Christmas holidays would begin the next day, and for that reason, Sherlock would have to come up with a little scheme. Neither Lupin nor I doubted our friend would succeed, but we didn't have the least idea what he would dream up.

While we waited for Holmes, Lupin did an excellent job avoiding any personal talk. Instead we chitchatted a little about the war and how we hoped it would end. There was a popular new government in Paris, but we both spoke of it with great suspicion. Then Lupin nudged me with his elbow and pointed at the school.

Sherlock had popped out at the top of the staircase, accompanied by a man in uniform, who walked him almost all the way to our carriage. Holmes then said goodbye to him, coughing heavily, and covered the distance that separated us with broad strides.

When he climbed into the carriage, our friend's appearance surprised us. His face was flushed, his eyes were shining, and his brow was beaded with sweat.

"You have a fever!" I exclaimed.

"Exactly," Sherlock announced perfectly calmly. "Thanks to the leaf of Virginia tobacco I ingested half an hour ago. Now, let's leave quickly," he added, "because the two of you aren't too convincing as Mama and Uncle, who came to pick up the poor sick student, and I don't want old Jenkins to notice something amiss."

Lupin laughed, amused, and told the coachman to continue straight for two blocks and then turn the corner. Once we were far enough away from St. Paul's School, however, Lupin ordered the coachman to stop in an open area, and he pulled a freshly printed copy of the *Standard* out of his pocket.

From the previous night's blurb in the paper, it was clear the news of the Twickenham murder had arrived shortly before the edition went to press, and, therefore, we expected more details in this new edition. But Lupin's quick scan did not add much to what we already knew, with one important exception: the exact address of Samuel Peccary's mansion.

"Number four Church Lane!" Lupin read aloud,

glancing at Sherlock, who immediately pulled the street guide from his pocket and began flipping through its pages feverishly.

"Aha!" Sherlock said a few moments later.

"A few more syllables would be welcome!" I said.

"A perfect correspondence," Sherlock said, with eyes that shined more with satisfaction than the fever alone could have produced. "The first of the Black Friar's codes is, indeed, V2 – P19 – D2. According to my interpretation, this means: second volume of the *Furlong Street Guide* of London, page nineteen, in the square on the map where D and 2 meet. Well . . . do you know precisely what is in that square?" he finally asked.

"Let's see if I can guess," said Lupin. "Church Lane, in the suburb of Twickenham!"

"Exactly," Sherlock confirmed.

"So that means —" Lupin began.

"I know what that means!" I interrupted without a second's hesitation. And I flung myself toward the tiny window used for communicating with the coachman. "Quick! Take us to Scotland Yard!"

The driver hesitated for a moment, but then he gave the reins a jerk and started the carriage. After traversing some side streets, we entered the chaotic traffic of Tottenham Court Road. The looks in my friends' eyes told me they agreed with my decision. The information we possessed was too important to hide from the police. And it didn't seem possible that what we had discovered was a simple coincidence. If we were correct in our hypothesis, two more people who lived at the addresses identified in the Black Friar's code were in mortal danger.

We reached our destination after about twenty minutes. Lupin paid the coachman, giving him a generous tip, and headed at top speed for the entrance of Scotland Yard, that oddly named building that housed the offices for the police.

We hadn't even reached the doorway when a tall, slouching police officer assailed us with his nasal, impolite voice. "Hey, kids! This is police headquarters, don't you know?"

"We know," replied Sherlock Holmes calmly. "But we have an important story to report."

The policeman was unimpressed and replied with arrogance, "If you have nice stories to tell, why don't you go to your neighborhood police station? I'm sure they'll be willing to listen to you."

"I have no doubt," Sherlock replied stubbornly. "But it so happens that what we have to say is too important for the neighborhood police!"

The policeman looked at us with a hostile air, deciding whether or not to believe us. "Then Officer Babcock will deal with you," he announced before he left, slamming the door.

Officer Babcock turned out to be a fat policeman with reddish-brown hair and watery eyes. Leaning over a dark wooden counter, he watched us with a bored air. "Listen, if you lost your doggie or a toy or something, you've come to the wrong place," he told us.

"The only thing we're in danger of losing is our patience!" Lupin said curtly. "So it's better for everyone if you listen to what we have to say."

"Oho!" said the officer, snickering. "I'm all ears."

"It's really important, sir," I intervened, looking him directly in the eyes. "It has to do with the murder of the man named Peccary in Twickenham."

The man in uniform behind the counter raised an eyebrow, a mixture of curiosity and doubt showing in his eyes. But since he seemed inclined to listen to what we had to say, I took that as a positive sign.

Sherlock and I traded looks, and my friend approached the counter. After pulling the newspaper clipping of the fake chess problem signed by the Black Friar from his satchel, he began to explain everything to Officer Babcock.

"When I saw this in the classified pages of the *Times* . . ." he began. And from there, with his analytical, penetrating manner, Sherlock went through all the details with the officer. He explained the true nature of the three brief codes in the fake chess problem, showed the match of the first code to the location where Peccary's murder had been committed, and then showed the officer the other two locations that were marked by the Black Friar's code.

When Sherlock finished his explanation, Officer Babcock, who up to that moment had not batted an eye, slammed his palms on the counter and opened his eyes wide. It came as a surprise to the three of us, but the policeman seemed to have been deeply struck by Sherlock's speech. This was confirmed when his beanpole of a colleague came into the office a few moments later.

"Carruthers!" the officer behind the counter

shouted. "These kids have discovered something interesting."

The second policeman seemed surprised. He locked eyes with his colleague. "How interesting?" he asked after a few moments of thoughtful silence.

"Quite interesting, I'd say!" Officer Babcock said. "A matter of secret codes that have to do with the murder in Twickenham, and the possibility of more murders still to come."

Officer Carruthers turned and looked at us suspiciously. "Secret codes, eh?" he repeated, turning back again to his colleague. "Worth disturbing Inspector Jarvis?"

The policeman behind the counter seemed to consider the matter carefully as he stroked his chin. "Yes, yes, I believe so!" was his final verdict.

Sherlock, Lupin, and I exchanged satisfied looks. We were succeeding in getting Scotland Yard on the trail of a dangerous killer!

"Follow me," said Officer Carruthers with a nod, leading the way. We didn't need to hear him a second time and followed him down a long, poorly lit hallway.

After climbing up a short set of stairs and

passing through another hallway, we reached a small, dark door. The policeman knocked lightly. Without waiting for an answer, he opened it and stood aside.

"After you," he prompted us. "Inspector Jarvis will be happy to receive you." And without adding another word, he disappeared into the halls of Scotland Yard.

My friends and I stepped through the doorway, surprised. The room was bare and tiny, and old chairs lined the walls. It wasn't at all how I'd envisioned the office of an important policeman of Her Majesty!

Even Inspector Jarvis's appearance seemed shabby. He was an elderly man, with white hair and bushy sideburns, and he was wrapped up in an old, dark, wrinkled coat.

I wondered if the clothes he wore were intended to disguise him as he infiltrated some gangster's den or conducted one of his other undercover investigations. The very idea thrilled me.

"Who sent you here?" Jarvis asked sharply, standing motionless beside the window, his eyes cast outside.

"Officers Babcock and Carruthers, sir," answered Sherlock politely, carefully watching the odd police officer. "They believe we possess some information that might interest you."

"I hope you do," Jarvis said gravely. "Anything that can help stop them is of the utmost importance!"

Sherlock, Lupin, and I looked at one another, surprised. Was there already an ongoing investigation? Was an entire group of criminals hiding behind the name of the Black Friar?

"Stop them? So there are already some suspects?" Lupin asked, expressing our astonishment.

The inspector turned and fixed two owl-like eyes on him. They sparkled with a vaguely unsettling light. "Anyone who isn't blind knows of their existence . . . the Dark Horsemen of the Apocalypse," he said. "They secretly plot to assassinate our queen . . . and when they succeed, nothing will prevent them from building the Evil Cathedral . . . "

When I think back to those moments after all these years, I cannot believe we didn't understand what was going on. But we were so naïve then, and we so honestly believed in our role as young investigators, that we spent I don't know how many minutes listening to the man's delusions.

When he raised his voice and declared,

"Humanity's days are drawing to a close!" we heard a guffaw from the hallway.

Sherlock and Lupin shot out of the room like hawks, leaving me alone with that poor old madman. I followed them a moment later, but in the short time that I stayed in Inspector Jarvis's room, he looked at me as if he were watching from another world and said, "I know exactly who you are."

And he gave me a look that froze the blood in my veins.

I raced out. In the hallway, I found the policemen from earlier, together with a small group that seemed to be having a great time.

"Idiots! You have no right to do this!" I hissed, full of rage. But that only made them laugh harder.

Sherlock was even angrier than I was. I saw his face flush until it turned purplish. He would surely have hurled his satchel at the policemen if Lupin hadn't wrapped his arms around Sherlock to stop him.

"Who the devil is the bloke in that room?" Sherlock demanded.

"Old Jarvis," answered one of the officers, trying to hold back his cackling. "He was one of us, but when he retired . . . let's just say that he lost a cog or two! Still, he's harmless, so we let him stay in an empty room — him and his conspiracy theories."

"Which are not very different from yours, my dear youngsters!" Babcock added, opening his eyes wide before bursting out laughing.

"So, were you listening?" Officer Carruthers asked.

"Oh, did he warn you about the coming of the Horsemen of the Apocalypse?" Officer Babcock quipped.

"You'll regret this! I can assure you, sirs!" Sherlock hissed, his eyes narrowing into slits.

"Hey!" Officer Carruthers said, turning to Lupin. "Your friend can't take a joke. Does he really want to threaten officers of Scotland Yard?"

"Joke, you say?" Sherlock repeated, trying to wiggle out of Lupin's grasp. "Maybe you haven't understood that your joke will cost someone's life."

"Oh, of course," Officer Babcock hooted. "They'll start by gunning down the queen, just as old Jarvis said!"

At that point, I saw Lupin push Sherlock toward the exit, making a sign to me to follow them. It seemed like an excellent idea to me, before we could get ourselves into bigger trouble than we could handle.

"You'll pay for this!" Sherlock screamed over his shoulder. "You'll come begging for my help! You'll come begging for it!"

Chapter 5

A TRIP TO TWICKENHAM

I don't think I would be mistaken in saying that the day's unpleasant episode left a deep impression on my friend Sherlock Holmes. Since then — and continuing to this day, from what I can tell — his attitude toward Scotland Yard has been marked by sharp distrust and obvious disdain.

After all, in those long distant days, we were three youngsters, full of pride and full of ourselves.

And these were the exact same feelings that made me honor my word to my mother. I had promised her I would help with the Christmas charity benefit run by her new group of London friends. Despite what Sherlock and Lupin might think and despite the new adventure we were about to embark on, I had decided that I would uphold my commitment.

My task consisted of sewing tiny dark buttons for eyes onto rag dolls. When I came home from visiting Scotland Yard, I took advantage of a moment when both my mother was away and Mr. Nelson was busy gathering wood for the house. I went to the sitting room where my mother kept the sack filled with the dolls, buttons, and a sewing kit, and took it to my room to hide it under my bed.

When I went back to my bedroom after dinner, I pretended I was going to sleep. Instead, I buckled down to the task of sewing buttons, one after another, onto the faces of dolls that would go to less fortunate little girls of London. While I was sewing under the halo of light from the oil lamp, I thought happily of how the girls might smile as they received these unexpected gifts.

I then let my thoughts wander to what my friends and I had discussed before parting. Due to the despicable behavior of the police, we had no choice but to continue our investigation into the Black

Friar's codes and the murder they seemed connected to — that of Samuel Peccary.

This new adventure would take place the next morning at ten o'clock sharp at Waterloo Station. After I had finished sewing eyes on all of the dolls, by which time it was almost dawn, I fell asleep with a smile on my face.

★ ★ ★

When I awoke a few hours later, I hardly thought of the sleep I'd lost. I returned the sack of rag dolls to the sitting room I had taken them from the night before. Then I waited until breakfast was over to tell my mother the work was already done — each of the dolls now had a pair of deep black eyes! Delighted by her amazed look, I got up and gave her a quick peck on the cheek.

"A promise is a promise, right?" I said. "And now I can focus on shopping for Christmas gifts. Yesterday I wasn't able to find anything acceptable on Portobello Road! Today I'll try again on Regent Street!" I said, imitating one of those posh girls from a good family that my mother so much wanted me to act like.

Mr. Nelson heard what I said and was waiting for

me at the door to the house with a carriage ready on the street.

After saying goodbye to my mother, I hurried down to the street and got in the carriage. "Quick! To Waterloo Station!" I said to the coachman, not hesitating a moment.

Mr. Nelson was sitting in front of me, watching silently, one of his sly smiles stretched across his face.

"Well?" I asked, smiling, as the carriage left.

"I should go to Regent Street, right?" he asked. "Shopping again, like yesterday?"

"Are you against that, Mr. Nelson?" I asked.

"Not at all . . . but I don't really know what to think this time. The last time you and your friends began something like this, Miss Irene, I had to take care to be sure nothing happened to you."

"This time is different, Mr. Nelson . . . " I replied.

"Perhaps because before beginning this new 'activity' with your friends, you thought about keeping your mother happy?" he asked.

"Not only that," I stressed. "It's different because there's no danger of any sort in the investigations we're undertaking."

"You said 'investigations,' Miss Irene," he noted.

I smiled, embarrassed. "I meant . . . activities."

"That's better," murmured Horatio Nelson, looking outside at the shop windows.

★ ★ ★

I said goodbye to Mr. Nelson and ran through the crowded arches of Waterloo Station. Lupin's gaudy crimson coat helped me find my friends in the throng of travelers.

"Hello, Irene!" my two friends greeted me in unison. Their two-voiced greeting was funny to me, and I allowed myself a brief laugh before replying.

To hide his embarrassment, Sherlock pointed to the large board that showed the schedules and said, "If we hurry, we can catch the 10:08 train!"

Lupin needed no repetition and sprang to a ticket counter that opened that very moment.

Without batting an eye, he ignored the muttering of the whiskered gentleman he had nimbly beaten to the punch, purchased three tickets for Twickenham, and gave them to us hurriedly.

"Thank you! Or should I perhaps thank that gentleman from Rotterdam?" I joked as we raced to get to our track.

"What does it matter, in the end? What's important is that we get where we're going, right?" Lupin answered, with one of those smiles of his that made him look like a naughty child.

Sherlock, though, said nothing. He simply led us toward the train that would take us to Twickenham. I realized my two friends must have reached some kind of unspoken pact: Lupin, who now had that large sum he had won gambling, paid for nearly everything without even being aware of it, and Sherlock let him do so without ever saying anything.

I scarcely had a few moments to ponder what might be wandering through the boys' minds before I had to concentrate on running to catch the train right away, its whistle already blowing, ready to depart.

* * *

We made it by a whisker. Lupin grabbed both my arms, helping me climb onto the steps of the train, and just then, I heard a puff of steam, along with the metallic clang of the wheels moving on the tracks. A few moments later, our train was leaving the station.

It had stopped snowing for several hours, and

now the rooftops of the city were all white. After at least a quarter of an hour of traveling southwest, we arrived in Twickenham, where a pale sun was trying to peek out from behind a thin layer of clouds.

Although it had now become a suburb of London thanks to the railroad, Twickenham still had the tranquil look of a rural village stretched out on the banks of the Thames.

Sherlock didn't even need to consult the *Furlong Street Guide*. "This way!" he said, stepping in front of us on the sidewalk along a wide, paved road.

After walking a few minutes, we found ourselves on Church Lane in an elegant area near the river. Along the sides of the road were the walls of several luxurious mansions. Bare tree branches rose over them here and there, veiled by a faint mist that rose from the Thames.

After a few steps, we heard confused yelling, which was jarring in this ghostly scene.

"Police again!" Lupin swore under his breath.

A few moments later, in front of the entrance to one of the mansions, I, too, glimpsed the dark outlines in the fog of several Scotland Yard policemen, with their dark coats and distinct helmets. All three of us hid behind a coal wagon parked on the side of the street.

"This must be the house of the victim, Peccary?" I asked.

"I'm nearly positive that this is number four Church Lane," replied Sherlock.

"Perhaps there's some news about the case!" Lupin suggested.

"That would certainly be good luck . . . getting here right now," I said.

"Our luck ends here, unfortunately," Sherlock said. "Whatever there is to discover is past the entrance, under police surveillance. And I don't think I need to remind you how little Scotland Yard seems to appreciate the help of three children."

"Maybe not, but there's nothing preventing us from at least taking a look," Lupin observed.

Sherlock and I agreed. Leaving our hiding place, we started walking along Church Lane again. When we passed by the mansion, we confirmed that Sherlock had been right. In front of the closed gate stood a crowd of policemen, who would thwart any attempts to get close to the house.

Taking care to maintain the casual attitude of

three everyday passersby, we turned toward the house, trying to see something. The Peccary mansion was a luxurious residence. It had a large garden surrounded by a number of manicured hedges.

"Look at the column to the left of the gate!" Sherlock suddenly whispered. I did as he said, and only then noticed a small yellow circle drawn with chalk on the column of blackened bricks.

Of course, it could have been an insignificant marking made by a bricklayer or some other worker. But to me, the thought that a murder had just been committed in this house gave that simple little yellow circle a disturbing air.

As we were marching along the other side of the street, trying to go unnoticed, we heard voices shouting from the grounds of the estate. Looking at one another in agreement, we darted around the corner and crouched against the wall to see what was going on.

I could actually see very little: two men, the younger one thin and with a neatly trimmed blond beard, and another, at least twenty years older. He had gray hair, a solid physique, and he seemed quite energetic. The two passed through the gate, engaged in what seemed like a heated discussion. The distance between us was too great for me to hear what they were talking about with such passion. But when I turned toward my friends, I saw a surprised expression on Sherlock's face.

"Did you see?" he asked, looking at us.

"I only saw two fellows arguing," I admitted.

"Me, too!" confirmed Lupin.

"Well, those are by no means merely 'two fellows,'" Sherlock explained. "The younger one must be the inspector in charge of the investigation while the other is Charles Frederick Field!" Sherlock spoke the name as if he expected Lupin and I would know whom he was talking about.

Our two pairs of wide eyes let him know that was not so.

"Field used to be the greatest detective in Scotland Yard," he explained. "He retired about ten years ago and became a private investigator."

"A private investigator?" Lupin repeated.

"In other words," I began, "someone who investigates without a partner?"

"Someone who investigates on behalf of whoever is ready to pay to find out the truth — if it can be found," Sherlock said. "An interesting new profession, wouldn't you say?"

"I'm not sure it would be right for me," Lupin said. "Anyway, the question now is: What the devil is Field doing here?"

"One thing's for sure. He's not working amicably with Scotland Yard! Those two were screaming at each other like banshees," I noted.

At my observation, Sherlock grew silent, lost in his thoughts.

Lupin, however, snorted. "Agreed," he exclaimed, getting to his feet. "It's time now to figure out something else."

Sherlock, realizing our friend was going back to Church Lane, grabbed his arm. "What are you thinking?" he asked.

"If it's a question of chess, secret codes, and the like, I'm not much help. But now I'm asking you to let me do what I do best," answered Lupin, a smile on his lips.

My two friends exchanged a long look. Sherlock released his grip on Lupin's arm, watching him cross the street and disappear into an alley that ran alongside the Peccary mansion.

When I saw Lupin's head poking out in the distance, on the other side of the wall that encircled the mansion, I jumped and grabbed hold of Sherlock's arm.

"Won't that be dangerous?" I asked.

"The part of the wall Arsène chose to leap over is hidden by that greenhouse," Sherlock said, pointing toward a glass and wrought iron roof that rose from the walls of the estate. "As long as he doesn't make any noise, the police shouldn't see him."

I tried to accept that cold, logical explanation, but my heart kept thumping wildly. I stood with my eyes glued to the small, distant speck that was Lupin's head. I saw my friend vault over the wall and admired his agility, which I thought must have improved in the last few months due to more frequent training with his father, Théophraste.

Taking off with another leap, Lupin clung to the branch of an oak tree, just like an acrobat grabs the trapeze bar. He balanced his weight nicely and jumped to the ground, disappearing from our sight past the wall.

Our friend seemed to have vanished into the fog that shrouded the Peccary mansion. At first I thought that was a good thing — that Lupin had managed to sneak in without attracting the attention of the police. But with each passing minute, the calm surrounding the place began to give way to a more anxious atmosphere. I squeezed Sherlock's arm while I searched in vain for a sign of Lupin.

I was seriously beginning to think about running to the other side of the street to go look for him when I suddenly heard a voice behind us.

"Are you waiting for someone?"

I jumped up and turned around, my hand on my heart, which almost leaped out of my chest from such a fright.

Before us stood Lupin, with a relaxed smile on his face. I shot him a nasty look.

"I thought it would be wiser to go around the block. There really are a lot of policemen around here. Sorry I scared you," he said.

"I'll forgive you if you give me some interesting news about what's happening," Sherlock joked.

Lupin rubbed the back of his neck thoughtfully. "It's funny," he finally said. "I haven't come back with empty hands, but . . . I haven't the foggiest idea what it all means."

Sherlock and I looked at each other, puzzled.

"Perhaps it's best if you tell us. Then we'll see," I suggested.

Lupin nodded and started his tale. "As soon as I got in there, I realized there were many more policemen than I'd thought. Trying to get into the mansion was completely out of the question. Even the service entrance in the back was guarded. So my one choice was to follow a path behind the greenhouse, which was the only safe route. I found out it led to the stables. Did you know that Peccary had some valuable thoroughbreds?"

"So now you're going to tell us about horses!" I said, getting back at Lupin for scaring me a few minutes earlier.

"No, sorry," Lupin replied, smiling. "If I do say so myself, I know a lot about that subject. But no. I met a stable hand and told him that I'd been sent there by a friend of Peccary, because I was looking to work in the stables."

"Excellent, Arsène!" Sherlock said, admiring how shrewd our friend was.

"I didn't actually hear very much," Lupin said. "He said I must have been given the wrong information, because they weren't looking for anyone. And then he mentioned the tragedy that had just struck his employer. I could tell he was a gossip and that I wouldn't have to pull the words out of his mouth. In fact, all I had to do was give him a bit of an opening, and he began talking on end —"

"And what did he tell you?" Sherlock asked.

"At first, nothing more than what we'd already learned from the newspaper. That Samuel Peccary, an apparently peaceful chap who minded his own business, was found in his study with a dagger in his back. But then, at a certain point, the stable hand looked around mysteriously, as if he was about to reveal the biggest secret on earth, and he whispered, 'On his desk, right next to his head, they found a rose. A scarlet rose!'"

That detail surprised me more than a little, and I gazed at my friend, wide-eyed.

"I looked at the stable hand exactly that way, too, Irene," Lupin said, frustrated. "Too bad that just as I was about to ask him to tell me more, I saw a pair of policemen appear, and I had to slip away!"

"Maybe that fellow was nuttier than old Jarvis!" I commented.

Lupin and I looked at each other, our eyes laughing. But when I turned back to Sherlock, I saw that his mood was completely different from ours. His eyes sparkled with a wild, shining light, as they did anytime something caught his attention. But what could have possibly struck him about what the stable hand had said?

"A scarlet rose . . ." Sherlock repeated, mumbling.

Without our noticing, the clouds above us had grown thicker. A freezing wind had begun to blow, bringing fresh snowfall with it. This time the flakes were fine and very dense.

"I think I have something to tell you!" Sherlock suddenly announced, emerging from the thoughts that had absorbed him. "But I'm afraid it won't be very pleasant in the midst of a storm . . . so follow me!" he finished, springing forward with his quick stride.

Lupin and I looked at each other, confused. Then we followed Sherlock.

Our friend retraced the route we had taken when we left the station until we reached an intersection. Then he stood there, looking around. "I thought I saw . . . there it is!" he exclaimed, pointing to a little old stone house at the end of the street, on the riverfront.

I looked over that way, too. Through the white veil of snow, I saw a large black sign that was squeaking, pushed by the wind. On it, we glimpsed the outline of a black ship, under which was written in yellow paint, At the Sign of the Old Brigantine.

Chapter 6

AT THE SIGN OF THE OLD BRIGANTINE

The Old Brigantine tavern was not much more than a big room filled with planks and stools, popular with fishermen and sailors. The fire burning in the large fireplace at the back of the pub and the small copper pots hanging from the walls made the tavern feel welcoming.

We settled in at a table near the hearth. After being outside in the cold, I enjoyed feeling the warmth on my skin.

Sherlock ordered a pot of hot tea. The innkeeper, a big man with a graying beard, gave us a suspicious look. But when Lupin dropped a handful of shillings onto the table, it seemed to be enough to satisfy him, because we saw him smile and head into the kitchen.

Sherlock waited until the man had served us the steaming tea. When it had steeped to a nice, dark shade, he poured it into all three of our cups and took a sip. Only then did he begin to speak. "That stable hand was in his forties at least, right?" he asked.

"Yes," Lupin confirmed. "The fellow looked fifty, more or less . . . but how did you know?"

"Simple. He wasn't a madman, as Irene suggested. He was just old enough to remember a few important events from the history of crime in this realm. Facts that, on the other hand, it seems you two are in the dark about," he concluded, looking at Lupin and me mockingly.

"Seeing that I'm not even a third the age of that man and have only lived in Great Britain for a few months, I believe my ignorance should be excused," I retorted.

"As for me, my knowledge of the history of crime is limited to the shining tradition of the Lupin family!" quipped Arsène.

Sherlock laughed, appreciating the joke, and

then had another sip of tea. "In any case, it won't be too hard to remedy," he continued. "The events in question date back about twenty years and have to do with an unusual group nicknamed the Scarlet Rose Gang. The name refers to the flower they would leave at the site of a crime as their 'signature.'"

"Oh. That explains the stable hand's excitement!" said Lupin.

"So why do you describe this gang of criminals as 'unusual?'" I asked.

"Great question, Irene," Sherlock said. "I could answer by saying that the Scarlet Rose Gang pulled off many daring heists and always came away with lavish loot: gem, gold ingots, valuable works of art. But that would be a mistake. What actually distinguished their activities was the great care with which they prepared for them. On one occasion, for example, they made sure they would get away by using a forgotten, old tunnel under the Hebrew cemetery on Alderney Road. Another time they managed to steal a Moldavian countess's priceless necklace by disguising themselves as agents from Scotland Yard. In other words, even though these gentlemen undoubtedly swung from the gallows, they are acknowledged as the first to have engaged in crime with a . . . scientific method."

"A scientific method?" I repeated.

"Quite so," Sherlock said. "When you read records of their criminal acts, it's clear that every one of their heists was based on a precise plan that was cleverly constructed down to the last detail."

"How many of them were there?" I asked.

"No one knows for sure. It seems there were at least four members in the gang. And it's said that each had a specific job, like gears in clockwork. Or at least, that was the conclusion of the Chief Detective in charge of the investigation then . . . Charles Frederick Field," Sherlock concluded, clearly enjoying this dramatic turn of events.

I let my eyes drift toward the weak light filtering through the fogged-up windows. The incident was taking on a clearer shape. Even our trip to Twickenham made sense: the large number of police deployed, Field's presence, the excitement of Peccary's stable hand over the detail of the scarlet rose found next to the corpse.

"So do you think the Scarlet Rose Gang has . . . come back?" I asked slowly.

Sherlock surprised me by answering immediately, although only partially. "If they're back in action, it can't be the original members of the gang."

"How do you know?" Lupin asked, perplexed.

"Because despite their abilities, they didn't get away with it," Sherlock answered. "Or at least the person who most likely was the head of the gang didn't get away. His name was Smeaton, if I remember correctly."

"Really? What happened to him?" I asked, pouring more tea for the three of us.

"What often happens. Fortune turns her back at the worst moment, it seems," Sherlock went on. "The gang was using an old toolshed along the Thames to hide the loot. They chose well. It was a very isolated spot that didn't stand out. But right after a dramatic heist of gold coins from a postal coach, someone passing by heard commotion inside the shed and sent an anonymous note to the police. Field and his detectives went to check. There they found some loot from heists that had been signed with the scarlet rose. They also found Smeaton's business card, which had apparently slipped out of his pocket. So they discovered it was an unsuspected worker from Her Majesty's Post who, at nightfall, was turning into the leader of the most feared gang of criminals in the area," Sherlock explained. "When the police showed up at Smeaton's house, he fled, but he was hit in the leg by a gunshot. They found him dead a few days later, in an alley near St. Giles. And ever since that day, there have been no more heists signed with the notorious scarlet rose."

"There have been no more . . . until today?" Lupin asked, astonished.

Sherlock nodded, and we were quiet for a while, sipping our tea and trading thoughtful looks.

"Listen to me for a minute," Lupin began after a bit. "From what you've told us, the old gang specialized in robberies. Very high-profile robberies."

"That's right," Sherlock confirmed.

"But this time, it's a murder. The *Standard* didn't mention that anything valuable had been stolen. Could the rose simply be a ploy to pull the wool over the eyes of the police?" Lupin argued.

"Possibly," Sherlock admitted. "Just as it's possible that the police, as well as the press, have kept other details secret, much like they hid the discovery of the scarlet rose."

"They're passing the news through a sieve," Lupin said, frustrated.

At that point, I pounded my fist on the table — a gesture that would have horrified my mother. "It's a shame!" I protested angrily. "We have very important information about this case, and no one will listen to us. And it's all just because of when we were born!"

Sherlock chuckled at my outburst. "Until a few hours ago, I felt very much the same way," he admitted. "But now I think what's happening is a marvelous Christmas gift to all of us."

His words stunned us.

"Enlighten us, please!" I urged.

"Think about it," Sherlock said, leaning toward us. "We offered the officers of Scotland Yard — on a silver platter! — facts that I'm willing to bet will be crucial to solving this mystery. Instead of thanking us, those idiots made fun of us. So do you know what I say? It's better this way. They've left an entire mystery for us to investigate!"

And with that, Sherlock pulled the all-important classified ad from the *Times* back out — the one that no one, besides the three of us, had paid any attention to.

Chapter 7

THE THREE BEGGARS

V1 – P47 – F5.

That was the second code in the Black Friar's fake chess problem. When I went back home that day, I ran to Papa's study. I remembered having seen the three thin volumes of the *Furlong Street Guide* on his bookshelves and was happy to discover they were indeed there.

Since the code began with V1, I pulled out the first volume of the set, following the method Sherlock had figured out. Then I sat down at the desk and flipped through the book until page 47, as shown by the second part of the code, P47. At that point, all that remained for me to do was find the square on the map that was located where F on the horizontal row met 5 in the vertical column.

My finger was pointing at Wimpole Street, where it intersected Queen Anne Street. It was a part of the city I knew, not far from our home, in the wealthy Westminster neighborhood.

Researching that spot on the city map wasn't the only thing that had awakened my curiosity. In fact, before we left the Old Brigantine, Lupin had pointed out that with all the comings and goings of the police in Twickenham, it would be foolish to try to continue investigations at the Peccary mansion. Instead, it was more urgent that we take a look at the second site on the Black Friar's list. Since the police at Scotland Yard hadn't taken Sherlock's theories seriously for even a moment, we could be sure we wouldn't have too many police underfoot there.

My research in the street guide confirmed what Sherlock had anticipated.

At my suggestion, we'd agreed to meet at Wimpole Street that evening at eight o'clock sharp. There was a reason I'd picked that hour. Due to a lucky coincidence, I had an excellent cover that evening. My singing teacher, Miss Langtry, had invited me to a small, private chamber music concert of near the Temple Bar.

At six o'clock sharp, following the Anglo-Saxon custom that our household had recently become accustomed to, dinner was served: *soup à la cantatrice,* marinated chicken, and rice. Still in a terrific mood, Mama updated me on her charity group's work for Christmas and how pleased they were with my rag dolls. I listened to her, a little ashamed to have to lie to her again, and then left the room to change clothes. Shortly after seven, I was ready.

Mr. Nelson accompanied me to the carriage as steady as a statue. I, on the other hand, was agitated. On the carriage ride, I talked and laughed a good deal, hoping to hide my anxiety. My plan relied on the heavy carriage traffic that blocked the roads around the Temple Bar at all hours.

The old gate of London was one of the busiest parts of the city. When I felt the coachman pull on the reins and heard him curse profusely at having to stop in the bottleneck of carriages, I smiled inside. The old, chaotic city of London had not let me down!

"My goodness!" I exclaimed, playing my part. "I'm going to be late to the concert! Miss Langtry will think I'm very rude." I grabbed the brass door handle.

Mr. Nelson leaned out the window and ordered the coachman to hurry, without any noticeable result.

"Listen, Mr. Nelson," I then said, seizing the opportunity. "It's the next street on the left. It will only take a minute by foot!"

And without waiting for him to answer, I opened the door to the carriage.

"Miss Adler!" the butler protested, reaching for my arm. But with a little leap, I was already on the sidewalk.

"Mr. Nelson, please don't nag," I begged, looking at him with a knowing smile. "I'll be sitting in my seat before you're moving again. See you later!"

"Sitting in your seat . . . are you sure about that?" the butler cried out.

I gave him a final wave and ran across the sidewalk, turning down the first street on the left, which really was the one that went to the building where the concert was being held.

But I never went to the concert. Instead, I hid behind a column and waited until the carriage with Mr. Nelson in it grew distant. I felt guilty about lying to him, which he certainly didn't deserve. But at least I'd given him a convincing excuse as to what had happened.

I had no choice, I told myself, swiftly walking away. Mama never would have agreed to let me leave the house if I'd told her what I wanted to do. I chose to take my liberty, by fair means or foul, and I wasn't sorry about that.

So after walking for a bit, I stopped a coach and hurried to my meeting. I got to Wimpole Street a few minutes late and found Lupin already there, waiting for me in the halo of light cast into the evening fog by a streetlamp.

"Good evening, Irene!" he greeted me. In the cold December air, his words became little clouds of smoke.

"Good evening," I greeted him back, pulling my coat tightly around me. I looked around, surprised not to see Sherlock, as I had grown accustomed to his clockwork punctuality. But my surprise did not last long.

Only a few moments later, we heard someone whisper from a nearby alley. Lupin and I looked at each other and then proceeded cautiously in that direction.

"Sherlock?" I asked, peering into the foul-smelling, dark alley.

By now I knew my friend Sherlock's eccentricity very well — eccentricity that just a few years later millions of people would come to know as well. But this time, the scene before me was truly bizarre. Sherlock's face was smeared with soot, he was wrapped up in a stinking old cloak that was at least a half a century old, and he was holding a frying pan riddled with holes and blackened from smoke.

"Good heavens!" Lupin exclaimed. "What the devil are you doing?"

"Can't you tell?" Sherlock replied, amused. "For the more than reasonable sum of a half sterling, I've just entered the roasted chestnut business!"

Lupin and I looked at him, afraid he'd lost his mind.

Sherlock enjoyed the expressions on our faces and burst out laughing. "Don't worry," he assured us. "I'm not doing it to make money. It's just that when I got here a little early, I noticed that this spot — where the roasted chestnut vendors stand — was perfect for taking a good look around."

"Wouldn't it be easier to simply pretend we're passersby?" I objected.

"Not this evening, unfortunately. In a bitter cold like this, passersby are few. Going back and forth on this stretch of the road would make us stand out, especially with that chap over there who's doing nothing but looking around all the time," he finished, pointing at a gray stone building.

At the entrance to the building, I saw a doorman dressed in a magnificent uniform, loaded with badges and gold stripes that gave him an important look. He was planted there like a sentry of sorts. All the windows in the house were lit, and I heard the sounds of a piano coming from inside.

It didn't take me long to understand that there was a party going on. I explained it to my friends. As was fitting in wealthy residences, in these situations, the doorman would wait at the entrance for guests.

"Well thought out, Holmes, really well thought out," Lupin said. He chuckled, patting Sherlock on the back as he poked at the dying fire he'd started.

I had to agree that Sherlock's idea was clever. Without hesitating, I took off my gloves so I wouldn't ruin them while helping my friends. We soon revived the small fire that was burning in the rusty old tub and put the chestnuts in the pan with the holes in it. Then — since Sherlock had also obtained another two filthy cloaks — I took a deep breath and threw one of those horrors onto my shoulders, telling myself I was doing it in the spirit of adventure.

In no time at all, the premiere establishment of "Holmes, Lupin & Adler – Roasted Chestnuts on the Promenade" opened its doors on the corner of Wimpole Street.

It was really cold, but the fact that it was late December was an advantage for us. Any other time of year, the presence of three beggars selling roasted chestnuts for a few pennies would not have been tolerated on a street like this one. Right before Christmas, however, the small fire on the street corner and the lovely smell of roasted chestnuts wafting through the air were happily accepted, even in the richest neighborhood in London.

Aside from a slightly drunk but peaceful fellow, we weren't able to attract many customers, but we at least had a way to watch this stretch of road. At a rough guess, the area we needed to survey was made up of six or seven homes on both sides of Wimpole Street, including the home having the party.

At first it was thrilling to be standing around a fire in the cold evening on a street corner with my two friends, playing the part of a beggar under those grimy cloaks. Even the smallest sounds and movements made my heart beat faster. The bark of a dog, a gentleman who paused to empty his pipe against a wall, a carriage that stopped in front of the building to drop off new guests.

I felt as if behind every person I saw there could be a crafty criminal and every instant could bring a surprise.

But nothing much changed. Dogs barked in the distance, the occasional pedestrian walked quickly along the sidewalk hurrying to get to the warmth of his house, and carriages with guests in evening dress stopped every once in a while in front of the gray stone building.

After spending a half hour this way, everything seemed perfectly ordinary to me: it was a cold December evening on a respectable London road.

At some point, Lupin grew bored, too. "The chestnuts are burning!" he announced. "And since we're dying of boredom, I say we should at least eat them ourselves." And with a blackened spoon Sherlock had bought from the beggars (along with all the other equipment), Lupin took a roasted chestnut from the pan and tossed it at me.

"Stop that!" Sherlock scolded. "We're stepping out of character. No roasted chestnut vendor would toss his own products into the air!"

"It just means we're the first acrobatic roasted chestnut vendors in London!" Lupin joked.

I remember those moments today as if I just lived through them. I laughed at Lupin's wisecrack as I tossed the red-hot chestnut from one hand to the other . . . and meanwhile brooded about how much time I had before I would have to be near the building where the concert was taking place for Mr. Nelson to find me. I only had around another twenty minutes, and it would take me twenty minutes to get back there.

It was right then we heard a shot.

It came from the lit-up building with the party.

My hands froze, as if turned to stone, and the

roasted chestnuts tumbled to the snow. Sherlock let the pan fall to the ground, and Lupin looked at both of us.

We heard a scream.

The door of a carriage parked down the road, which we'd thought was empty, burst open.

The doorman rushed into the gray stone house.

"Come on! Let's go!" Lupin urged us, running across the deserted street.

Sherlock immediately joined him. I hesitated for an instant, but then I caught up with them.

We had barely begun running toward the building when we heard a racket from the back of the house. A door forcefully banged shut, and we heard footsteps that sounded like someone was running.

"This way!" Lupin shouted, changing direction unexpectedly.

Following him, we slipped into a narrow alley that led to the back of the building. As we were passing the corner of the building, I glimpsed, for a moment, a circle drawn with yellow chalk on one of the large stones in the wall.

It was identical to the one we had seen at the gate of the Peccary mansion in Twickenham.

I didn't even have time to be startled. I had to race to avoid having my friends leave me behind — the last thing I wanted to happen!

"I saw someone running away!" Sherlock yelled, pointing to the corner of an alley that was bathed in shadows.

From that moment on, everything became chaotic. The back door to the building opened. Out ran the doorman and another man in evening dress.

"Hey, you!"

"Stop!"

The two shouted and launched themselves toward us.

It was only then that I realized just how dangerous this situation was. Something bad had just happened in that house, and the doorman and the other man thought that the three of us were involved!

"Run!" shouted Sherlock, grabbing my arm hard.

I didn't think about anything else and did what he'd told me to do. I ran as fast as I could, while the shouts of our pursuers thundered through the alley and my heart beat like a crazed drummer.

Lupin, the fastest of us, was a few feet ahead when he suddenly stopped and pointed at a nook that was plunged in total darkness, inviting us to hide there with him. We flattened ourselves against the cold, damp surface of the wall and held our breath.

I felt Sherlock's heart beat wildly against my face and realized that the young Holmes was clutching me in a firm embrace. We heard our pursuers draw near, shout something, and then continue onward.

Lupin's hiding place had worked!

We waited for a few moments and then, almost hesitating, Sherlock released his grip on me. The three of us then ran in the opposite direction and popped out again on Wimpole Street, convinced we had escaped. But instead, we found the street cut off by a carriage, the same one that had been parked near us the entire evening.

"Watch where you're going!" Lupin yelled, without thinking.

A door opened, and out stepped a solid man with a craggy face; a long, dark coat; a black bowler hat; and a long pistol pointed toward us. I recognized him immediately. It was Charles Frederick Field.

Chapter 8

A GREAT DETECTIVE

"You three, put your hands up high in the air!" the former Chief Inspector of Scotland Yard ordered us. "And don't even think about making the slightest move, or it will go worse for you!"

I felt a mixture of anxiety and fear grip my throat. But since my friends had been caught unaware and couldn't seem to utter a word, I found my courage and spoke up.

"It's not . . . not what you think, Mr. Field," I said as loud as I could.

The investigator was silent, as if surprised to hear

a girl's voice. I took advantage of his confusion and continued speaking.

"We had nothing to do with that shot . . ." I said. "We were only out here to carry out a little . . . investigation."

"Take two steps back toward the streetlight," he ordered. "I want to see you better."

We did as he said. After he'd looked at us thoroughly, verifying we were actually three children, he seemed even more surprised than before. "I didn't think I had any competition this young in the investigative field . . ." he began. "And goodness only knows why, but I find it easier to believe that's what you are, rather than three delinquents who have fallen into a heap of trouble far bigger than they are!"

At that moment, from behind the gray stone building, we heard the thundering cries of our pursuers again, doubling back on their own steps. We had only seconds left, and our only hope was to convince Field we were telling the truth. I needed to speak very quickly and convincingly.

But instead, falling prey to anxiety, I said the first thing that came to mind. "You have to believe us, Mr. Field! We came here because . . . we discovered clues in the *Times* . . . hidden information, strange codes concealed in a chess problem. But the officers at Scotland Yard didn't believe us, and then . . ."

My words petered out as I realized I'd just produced the weakest and most absurd speech ever to leave human lips.

You can imagine my astonishment then when I heard Field's voice inviting us to jump into his carriage instead. "Go on, quick! Get in! If those fellows nab you, you're done for."

We didn't make him say it a second time. After tossing the filthy beggars' capes to the ground, we leaped into the carriage alongside Field, who ordered his coachman to leave at a gallop. Once we felt the carriage begin to move, the three of us sat back against the seats, sighing in relief.

We stayed quiet, listening to the cracking of the whip and the sound of the wheels on the cobblestones. Then Sherlock spoke, his voice perfectly calm. "Mr. Field, I know you've gotten us out of a huge problem, and I don't want to appear reckless now . . . but may I ask how you figured out the secret code in the fake chess problem signed by the Black Friar?"

The detective seemed to be about to answer. But

then he scowled and asked in turn, "Young man! How do you know I broke that strange code?"

"It's simple, Mr. Field," Sherlock began. "Without taking anything away from my friend's speechmaking abilities, it's clear that it was her reference to a code that appeared in the pages of the *Times* that convinced you she wasn't lying. And that only makes sense if you also know what it's about."

"Your reasoning makes sense, son," Field started. "And indeed, that's the case. We were in the same place for the same reason — that cursed message in code that appeared in Monday's *Times*! Although, to tell you the truth, I did not solve that riddle personally."

"Who was it, then?" Sherlock asked.

"One of my young associates," Field explained. "A very intelligent young man, albeit a bit odd, who's been acting as my secretary several hours a week. He's so reserved and silent that I call him the Shadow. Anyway, it was he who came up with the coded message that, according to him, referred to several sites in the London street guide . . . Ah!" Inspector Field seemed to glimpse something outside the window, was silent for a moment, and then continued. "Now, however, if you don't mind, it's my turn to ask you some questions! To start, I'd like to know whom I have the pleasure of meeting, and particularly, how the devil you three wound up in the middle of this ugly business!"

After introducing ourselves, Sherlock, Lupin, and I each took a turn summarizing everything that had happened up to that evening honestly, without leaving out any details. The investigator listened to everything we said with great interest, but I saw his eyebrows arch in surprise when Lupin explained to him that we also knew about the detail of the scarlet rose found at the scene of the crime in Twickenham.

At the end of our explanations, Field shook his head and chuckled in disbelief. "Now if you were my own children, I'd give you a first-rate scolding, but I can't deny that you've done excellent work," he admitted.

"Speaking of work . . . " Lupin said, seizing the opportunity. "May we trouble you to ask why you're pursuing this investigation? From the discussion we saw you having with that officer, Scotland Yard doesn't seem to appreciate your help — just as it didn't like ours!"

Field sighed deeply. It was obvious that Lupin's question had brought unpleasant thoughts to his mind.

"At first, it was just a detective's misgiving," the investigator answered. "My young associate showed me the possible lead to a crime, and I merely kept my eyes open. But then the Twickenham murder took place, and an old colleague, Sergeant Wells, disclosed the detail of the scarlet rose on Peccary's desk to me. That changed things. According to what you've told me, it seems as though you know the old story of the Scarlet Rose Gang. So you would also know that at that time, when I was still Chief Inspector of the police, I only managed to get my hands on the ringleader, a man named Smeaton. Ever since, I've considered it unfinished business between the rest of the gang and myself, and I won't leave any stone unturned to try to settle that score!"

"No one knows if this mysterious affair really involves the old gang," Inspector Field continued, "but I was hoping Inspector Babbington would be willing to join forces to try to uncover the truth. Well . . . I was sadly mistaken! That young cop is a vain man, and he's afraid I will steal his glory. And so here

I was this evening on my own, full of doubts as to whether I was following an investigative trail or just a simple blunder. But that gunshot and then meeting the three of you — now every doubt I had is gone. Something very real is hidden in the coded message from this mysterious Black Friar!"

All the explanation from Mr. Field had distracted me from the drama of what had just occurred.

"What do you think happened in that house on Wimpole Street?" I then asked.

"Your guess is as good as mine. But that pistol shot is not a sign of anything good," Field answered in a grave tone. After those words, the carriage fell silent.

As I tried to push away the shiver that ran down my spine like an evil serpent, I noticed Sherlock's eyes twinkling in the shadows. I could tell he was enjoying himself immensely!

"Mr. Field," he said with obvious excitement, "under the circumstances, don't you think we should join forces to conduct this investigation?"

Field frowned in reply. "Young man, I always prefer to speak honestly," he began. "And that's why I'm asking you, why should a professional detective think that three little amateur children, however brilliant, could be of assistance to him, instead of bringing him lots of trouble?"

There was no denying that from Field's point of view, it was a real concern. And perhaps for that reason, my friend Sherlock did not know how to respond.

At that moment, a lightbulb went off in my head, and I realized that I had an ace up my sleeve. "Well, for example, you might discover that those 'little amateur children' would be in a position to provide your investigation some valuable clues," I said, taking courage.

"Ah, right . . . and what clues might you be suggesting, miss?" Field answered, uncertain.

"Any kind. How about, for example, that little circle in yellow chalk?" I responded.

I played my ace and told Field about the small circular mark I had seen on the wall of the building on Wimpole Street — identical to the one I had seen at the Peccary home this morning.

Field was amazed, as were Sherlock and Lupin — they, too, were learning about my big discovery that very moment.

The detective slapped the leather seat. "What on earth!" he exclaimed. "Well, I know when to admit I've been outsmarted . . . even when it's done by a young maiden who's as lively as a butterfly!"

And without another word, he handed Lupin — who was sitting across from him — his business card.

Chapter 9

FLEET STREET SCOOPS

I've never been one to use dramatic expressions, but I must say I awoke the morning after the events on Wimpole Street feeling that our clean getaway the night before had been a real miracle!

Field's carriage had taken me near the Temple Bar, at the exact corner where I'd waved goodbye to Mr. Nelson not long before, and in that same spot a few minutes later, our butler returned to pick me up in another carriage.

On the way home, Mr. Nelson asked if I'd enjoyed the concert. Making use of my musical knowledge, I described the strengths and weaknesses of a concert I'd actually never attended. Mr. Nelson stayed silent, and in a short while, we were back home.

The next morning, I went down to the sitting room in an excellent mood, thinking that perhaps the old saying, "Fortune favors the bold," was true.

I found my mother seated at the breakfast table. She was very happy, too, and, after a sip of tea and a piece of buttered toast (bacon and fried eggs were a local custom she never grew accustomed to), told me about the strange English tradition of making Christmas pudding with a penny hidden in it. The person who finds the coin between his teeth is supposed to have good luck in the year to come.

"I don't see how breaking a tooth by biting into a penny can be considered lucky!" I commented, making my mother laugh.

Our breakfast ended pleasantly like this. But when Mr. Nelson entered the room to clear the table, I noticed something wasn't right. He greeted me respectfully but coldly, without meeting my eyes.

A few minutes of this were enough to confirm my suspicion. There had been no miracle the evening before. I hadn't gotten away cleanly, as I had thought.

As soon as I had a chance, I went up to him. "Mr. Nelson, is there something wrong?" I asked.

"Since servants have to be loyal to their masters and not vice versa, there's nothing wrong, Miss Adler," the butler replied to me, continuing to clear the table without looking at me.

"Mr. Nelson, I . . . I don't know what . . ." I stammered.

"You need not put on an act, miss," he said. "Last evening, your behavior struck me as odd. After you got out, I stopped the carriage to watch you. So I know perfectly well you did not go to a concert."

Next to me was a mirror, and I saw my face suddenly flushing in humiliation, as if I were a child caught stealing jam. The very idea of having betrayed Mr. Nelson's trust so dramatically made me feel ill.

"I'm sorry for lying to you, Mr. Nelson," I said. "But the fact is, my friends and I found ourselves in the midst of a very complicated matter. At first we behaved properly, but no one would pay attention to us, and so —" I said, trying to justify my actions.

"You don't have to defend yourself, miss. If anything, think of the wrong you do your parents by behaving irresponsibly," Mr. Nelson replied.

"You won't say anything to my mother or father, will you?" I asked, hiding my face.

"It's not my habit to tell tales, and I will not do so, not even in this situation. From now on, however, I ask that you treat me as what I am — a mere servant and not your accomplice," Mr. Nelson said.

Those words hit me like a jab in the stomach. Nevertheless, I tried to behave calmly and nodded, avoiding Mr. Nelson's eyes.

"Very well," I said. "Then I would like you to prepare the carriage to take me to Carnaby Street."

Mr. Nelson nodded and took his leave with a deep bow, almost as if he wished to make it clear that he had really gone back to being an ordinary butler.

Of course, he was still much more than that to me, but I had no way to make him understand it at that moment. So I pushed down the lump in my throat and went to my bedroom to get ready.

★ ★ ★

Before going into the Shackleton Coffee House, I bought a newspaper from a paperboy on the corner of the street. Despite feeling anxious to do so, I glanced at the first page.

A headline made my heart sink: "Mysterious Murder on Wimpole Street."

My eyes devoured the short article that followed the headline, and I learned that just as in Twickenham, a homicide had been committed in the building we'd been watching the evening before. The victim was Joseph Barrow, a rich businessman in his fifties. The article did not give additional details about what had happened, however.

This proof of just how dark and terrible an incident my friends and I had stumbled upon the night before — combined with what had just occurred with Mr. Nelson — upset me more than I wished to admit. So I walked into the café with a heavy heart.

What I saw as soon as I entered, however, was so intriguing that I managed to shake off my grim mood, at least partly.

Sherlock and Lupin were seated at our regular table with a thin little boy who had red hair and bright-green, shrewd eyes. He couldn't have been more than ten years old, and I wondered what had brought him to my friends' table.

Before meeting my eyes, Sherlock's intense, flickering gaze rested on the newspaper I held under my arm, letting me know that he and Lupin were aware of the Wimpole Street murder.

"Welcome, Irene!" he said, pouring me a cup of cocoa. "I have the pleasure of presenting Mr. Scott Mullarkey to you or — as everyone knows him on Fleet Street — Sparky," he finished. The little boy with red hair greeted me with such a deep bow that it almost seemed he was teasing.

"Pleased to make your acquaintance, Scott Mullarkey," I said.

"It would seem that young Sparky is a valuable addition to our bold band of busybodies!" joked Lupin, giving the boy a light pat on the back.

I looked at the boy's sassy, bright-green eyes again. "Give me a likely reason," I said, "and I'll be willing to believe you." I sat down between them. I wanted Sparky to understand that even though I was a girl, I knew how to poke fun, too.

But Sherlock, it seemed, wanted to plunge headfirst back into the investigation. He immediately began to speak. "It all started with an elementary observation," he explained. "A quick scan of the city papers revealed an interesting fact. The articles on the Peccary murder are nearly identical to those on the other one. Everything is vague, and especially curious . . . there's no mention of the scarlet rose."

"Journalists aren't what they used to be?" I guessed.

"That's exactly the point: journalists normally wouldn't let such a sensational detail slip," Sherlock explained. "A headline on the possible return of the Scarlet Rose Gang could sell thousands of copies on its own!"

"And instead . . ." said Lupin, thoughtfully.

"Instead . . . silence!" Sherlock exclaimed. "A silence that smells like a rat from a mile away. And so here's where Sparky comes in. He's the fastest, most agile errand boy on all of Fleet Street, and he's also the best eavesdropper I've ever met!"

Fleet Street was the road where all the London daily newspaper offices were located, and Sherlock, who had already been contributing his successful riddles column to the *Globe* for a few months, explained that he'd met Sparky in the paper's chaotic corridors.

The little boy made a second comical bow and took the floor. He had the alert air of someone who had grown up on the streets but also a surprisingly polished way of speaking. He was a strange character to say the least.

"Mr. Holmes asked me to keep my ears open about this affair in Twickenham. So I did," he reported. "In all honesty, it's the easiest shilling I've ever earned. It's practically the only thing people talk about in the newspaper hallways, albeit softly!"

With a wave of his hand, Sherlock invited the boy to continue.

"Nothing like this has ever happened in the past," Sparky went on. "Inspector Babbington of Scotland Yard secretly summoned all the editors from Fleet Street to give them a very clear message . . . "

At this point, the boy looked around carefully to make sure no one else was listening to our conversation, and, leaning across the table, he whispered, "Nothing must leak out about these new crimes by the Scarlet Rose Gang! Whoever disobeys this order will be charged with no less than treason to the Crown!"

A low whistle escaped Lupin's lips. "Oh, boy!" he said. "Treason to the Crown . . . that's a serious matter. Those reporters will be frightened by that threat, eh?"

"A disturbing threat," Sherlock said. "Seeing that no one has stepped out of line."

I, too, was stunned by Sparky's story. "I wonder what pushed Scotland Yard to decide that?" I asked.

"To answer your question, I think you should consider what happened twenty years ago, when the gang was at the peak of its fame," Sherlock responded. "Driven by more and more colorful, fantastic tales in the papers, London was overcome by a sort of citywide insanity. Every day, hundreds of people overwhelmed police stations with false reports. One fellow even shot an innocent flower seller in Charing Cross, convinced he was the ringleader of the gang. As if that wasn't enough, many criminals who had nothing to do with the gang began depositing scarlet roses at the sites of their crimes in order to muddy the waters and confuse the investigation. In other words, it became almost impossible for Scotland Yard to track down the real Scarlet Rose Gang."

"But in the end, they nabbed the leader — Smeaton," Lupin said.

"That's true," Sherlock said, "but that was largely a stroke of luck. For the reasons I just mentioned, the police had been ignoring reports and anonymous messages that mentioned the Scarlet Rose Gang. Instead, the note that led them to Smeaton's toolshed on the Thames only spoke of suspicious movements and a possible den of thieves. Although it may seem strange, it was precisely the vagueness of that report that allowed the police to strike at the Scarlet Rose Gang," Sherlock said, indulging in a sip of cocoa.

"But the ambitious Babbington doesn't seem to want to wait for a stroke of luck this time," I said. "It's clear he's hoping this case will make his career."

Lupin nodded. Then he stretched against the back of his chair and looked at Sparky. "And you? Is that all the information you made off with?" he asked.

"Not at all, sir," the boy replied, pursing his lips. "No one on Fleet Street dares break the silence the police imposed," he continued. "But there are things whispered in the corridors, even if they don't wind up in the papers, and —"

"And your well-trained ears snatched them all, like butterflies in a net!" I interrupted. "So the time has come for you to whisper them in our ears, dear Sparky."

The boy clearly was not accustomed to being treated with such boldness by a young lady of good society. His cheeks turned red. But because he was an alert little fellow, he continued.

After asking us to come closer, he said, "To begin with, last evening on Wimpole Street, a scarlet rose was found at the scene of the murder, too. And then, in both cases, a theft accompanied the murder . . . in Twickenham, a dagger with a gem-studded handle, and on Wimpole Street, a pin that the victim was wearing on his collar."

Sherlock, Lupin, and I exchanged glances. In both cases, a valuable object had been stolen. I couldn't help but notice that this seemed like an important similarity to the robberies committed by the Scarlet Rose Gang twenty years before.

"Do they know if these objects were really that valuable? Enough to prompt someone to commit two murders?" asked Lupin, getting to the heart of the matter.

The young errand boy spread his hands. "Sorry, Mr. Lupin," he said. "I'm afraid only the investigators at Scotland Yard have that knowledge."

In any case, Sparky had done good work. In addition to the shilling Sherlock paid him, I offered to pay for a cup of hot cocoa for him.

The little boy gulped down the drink, delighted. After bowing to us in his funny way, he left us to our troubled thoughts.

"And now what do we do?" I asked after a few minutes, unable to stand the silence.

As if awakened by my voice, Sherlock emerged from his thoughts. He pulled the small volume of the *Furlong Street Guide* from his pocket, opening to where he'd put a thin strip of paper in as a bookmark. "V2 – P31 – C2," he said as he placed it on the table.

That was the third line of the Black Friar's coded message. Lupin and I, who were familiar by now with identifying the Black Friar's code, deciphered it together.

"Volume two."

"Page thirty-one."

"Square C2."

"Precisely," Sherlock said, putting a finger on the map. "Which corresponds to a stretch of Ladbroke Square."

Taking another look at the map, I saw that Ladbroke Square was a street in the Notting Hill district — another elegant part of London.

"The only thing we now know for sure is that

someone in this square will soon have a less than pleasant visit," Lupin said.

"That's true! We must go there! I bet we'll find the usual yellow chalk circle on the wall of a house there!" I said, excited. "We have to alert those who live there. You know how the last two times ended!"

Sherlock laughed bitterly. "Certainly . . . three children with a strange theory based on a chess problem published in the *Times*, a mysterious small circle drawn in chalk, and scarlet roses. Do you think anyone would believe it wasn't just a prank?"

What Sherlock said was as discouraging as it was true. For the umpteenth time, we'd collided with reality. Our ages were what prevented the dull adult world from taking us seriously . . . how infuriating!

All three of us sank back into our chairs in frustrated silence until Lupin smoothed his jacket and sighed. "If we do it all ourselves, yes!" he exclaimed. "But we're no longer merely three children. Now there's someone who is willing to listen to us!"

And with the same gesture a player might use to drop the winning card, Lupin made an ivory-colored slip of paper appear between his fingers: Inspector Charles Frederick Field's business card.

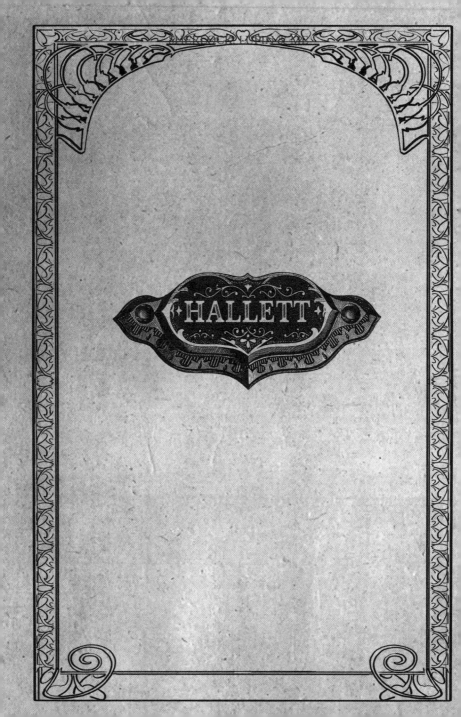

Chapter 10

A SUDDEN CHANGE

If there's one lesson I've learned about the unpredictability of life, it happened on that seventeenth day of December, 1870.

Indeed, as I sat in a shabby armchair at the Shackleton Coffee House with Sherlock and Lupin, I could not foresee the mysterious events that would occur later that day.

We all simply gazed at the detective's business card. There was no need for words.

By a happy coincidence, the address of the investigator's office was on Oxford Street, not far from the coffee house. If we hurried, I could go with my friends before getting back to the café in time to meet Mr. Nelson. So all three of us rose at once, as if moved by a secret force, and left the café hastily.

The sun had just managed to push through the huge, ragged clouds, and we walked quickly under the bright, glaring light. In less than ten minutes, we were on Oxford Street, opposite the entrance of a somber building with two white columns in front. One of the small marble signs alongside the main entrance read:

CHARLES F. FIELD

PRIVATE INVESTIGATOR

Third Floor

We entered the building without hesitating and climbed the stairs to the third floor. We glanced at the brass nameplates on each door until we found Inspector Field's office. Lupin grabbed the door knocker hanging from the mouth of a fierce bronze lion and struck three loud blows. To our surprise, the door sprang open immediately, opened by Field himself.

He stood in front of us, wearing his coat and carrying a walking stick and a hat in his hands.

"Here are my young guardian angels! Good day," he greeted us, in a playful tone of voice. "I cannot say that you lack the timing of great detectives," he continued, holding up his hat and walking stick. "Two minutes later, and you would've missed me."

"Well," Sherlock began boldly, "it would seem to me that you're in a great hurry to pay a visit to your old friends at Scotland Yard."

Lupin and I looked at him, wide-eyed and embarrassed, which was nothing compared to the flabbergasted expression Field gave him.

"And how did you —" he started.

"One merely needs to keep one's eyes open!" Sherlock said quickly, in order to reduce the investigator's embarrassment. "You can't miss that small gold pin depicting a mastiff, which you're wearing on your collar. If I'm not mistaken, veterans of Her Majesty's police wear it, and I'm certain you weren't wearing it in the carriage yesterday evening. Clearly you're going to a place where that pin can produce some effect, be useful for something . . . and that place can only be Scotland Yard."

Field closed the door and stopped to look at Sherlock, impressed. "Well done, young man. Very well done," he said. A smile spread across his face. "You remind me of my young associate, only you're a little more cheerful than he is. Ha, ha! I'd like to introduce you to him one day, don't you know?" Mr. Field added, looking at my friend one last time.

Sherlock nodded, mumbling something. I sensed he was a little embarrassed and disappointed to be compared to another boy the same age.

"You won't consider me foolish if I ask why you're visiting Scotland Yard, right?" Lupin asked, getting straight to the point as usual.

"Not at all," Field calmly answered. "As of yesterday evening, we're partners of a sort, aren't we?" he said. "And as partners, you're permitted to know why I'm going to Scotland Yard. It is because I've decided to get them to listen to me once and for all, even if I have to ram all the information I possess into Babbington's hard head!"

"Even after what happened before?" I couldn't keep myself from asking.

At that point, the investigator sighed deeply. "It wasn't easy to make this decision," he admitted. "Ever since Babbington refused my aid, I've told myself he could go to the devil! But now . . ." he continued, pausing slightly to point to the newspaper he held under his arm, "there have been two homicides in this ugly business. Perhaps I should put aside my personal pride and help the police carry out the investigation as efficiently as possible. And if they don't want me to contribute, well . . . I shall obey. I'll have to swallow my pride, but it won't be the first time. After all, I'm just an ex-policeman . . . no one knows that better than I do."

When Field had finished speaking, I looked at my friends. There was a little disappointment in their eyes. If things were as Field said, our adventure would soon be finished, and it would become an official police investigation. I'd be lying if I said I didn't feel disappointed, but it only lasted for an instant. In fact, I was the one who, two days before, had insisted we go to Scotland Yard to show them what we'd discovered.

Underneath it all, I thought, *we're all on the path to the same goal.*

Charles Frederick Field warmly shook hands with all three of us and bid us farewell, taking the stairway.

★ ★ ★

I must confess that although I felt disappointed at first, I was actually relieved that I would be able to enjoy this marvelous London Christmas. I was determined to get those two spoilsports — Sherlock and Lupin — to embrace the Christmas spirit.

The three of us said goodbye in the street outside Field's office, agreeing to meet the next day, and I went back home in the carriage with Mr. Nelson.

Our butler continued to make a show of being distant from me. But I had an idea. Even though it would be completely against my mother's standards of etiquette, and she would surely turn her nose up at it, I would buy a Christmas present for Mr. Nelson to show him I was sorry!

So that afternoon, I walked along the busiest streets in the city, frittering away my time thinking of a gift idea for Mr. Nelson.

Thanks to the *Furlong Street Guide,* which I'd borrowed from Papa's study, and a stroke of good luck, I came upon the perfect gift in the window of a small Bond Street jewelry store that sold charming necklaces and trinkets in every shape and size. It was there that I found a pendant shaped like an

American Indian hatchet. I imagined it had been buried underground to ratify the peace between two tribes. I thought it a clever gift and bought it without a second thought.

To my great surprise, when I returned from my trip to the shops, I found Sherlock waiting for me in front of my home. His face was strained and his expression nervous. He ran to meet me, and skipping the usual pleasantries, began to speak agitatedly. "Irene, I'm afraid there are problems on the horizon."

I wondered whatever could have happened, and I looked closely at Sherlock. He grabbed my hand, squeezing it for a moment, and then right after — as if he realized that it might be bothering me — he let go of it.

"A little while ago, Field's old friend, Sergeant Wells, came to the Shackleton Coffee House to find me. Things didn't go as expected. As soon as Inspector Babbington learned that Field had been near the Barrow home before the police arrived, he had him thrown in a jail cell for interfering with the investigation. He didn't even give Field time to pass on the information that he'd wanted to share!"

"But that means that —" I began.

"It means we're back at the beginning, Irene," Sherlock said. "After all that's happened, Scotland Yard will continue to ignore the trail of the Black Friar. Thus the third designated victim, the one from Ladbroke Square, won't have any protection or warning. He'll be completely ignorant and defenseless before the danger that is about to come upon him."

"I don't know why you're acting so hopeless. If the police don't do it, we can go and guard this person!" I argued.

Sherlock grimaced, disappointed. Then he laughed bitterly. "Apparently, fate wants to remind us who we really are today — that is," he said, "three children."

"Holmes, will you stop speaking in riddles?" I said, frustrated.

"All right, Irene. This is what's going on: Lupin has just been reunited with his father. They are shut away at a hotel, arguing furiously. I wouldn't rule out the possibility that before the evening is over, Théophraste will take Lupin back to the circus with him. As for me, I've been given the honor of working as a nurse. My little sister, Violet, has fallen ill with a high fever, and because my mother is at work and my brother Mycroft has returned to Cambridge, I must tend to her, at least until this evening."

It was not difficult for me to understand how much it must have bothered Sherlock to tell me these details, which he surely found humiliating.

"I'll try to leave when my mother returns home," he said. "I'll go around Ladbroke Square, hoping that the worst won't have already happened. It's the only thing I can do."

He waited a few seconds and then looked at his pocket watch. After a frustrated sigh, Sherlock said goodbye to me, hurrying to get home.

I remained in front of my house for some time before going in.

I can't hide the fact that my friend's behavior had hurt me. The idea that I could go to Ladbroke Square to warn the person in danger didn't seem to have even crossed his mind. Or perhaps I had misunderstood his silence and agitation? Maybe I should have suggested that I go in his place.

My thoughts immediately went to Hilda, the courageous circus girl who Lupin so admired. Was I really less brave than her?

With an abrupt decision so typical of youth,

I immediately resolved to prove the opposite. I pulled my coat around me, and instead of going up the stairs, I began to walk again, leaving my home behind me.

★ ★ ★

I reached Notting Hill thinking only of the beating of my heart, which was getting louder and louder.

Ladbroke Square was a well-ordered grid of paved roads that framed a lovely garden asleep beneath the snow. The buildings overlooking the square were elegant, immersed in the quiet of a street without shops and stores. I took the second volume of the *Furlong Street Guide* out of my pocket and headed toward the corner of the square that had been indicated by the Black Friar's coded message.

Once there, I let my steps slow and my eyes linger over the entrances of the buildings. Columns; small statues; marble steps; low, dark brick walls . . . and right on one of the thick pillars alongside some entry steps, hidden in a corner, I saw a small, yellow chalk circle, identical to the one I'd spotted in Twickenham and on Wimpole Street.

It was exactly what I was looking for. As soon as I glimpsed it, I caught my breath and froze.

A man's brusque voice broke the spell.

"Hey, miss! What on earth's the matter?"

The words came from the last step of the short stairway marked with the yellow chalk circle.

If I hadn't been disturbed by a thrill of fear, I would have noticed how comical the situation was. I'd seen a tiny sign drawn in chalk at the foot of the stairs, but I hadn't even been aware of the two huge men standing a few steps up, in front of the door to the building!

I took care of that right away, giving them a good look. They were both tall and sturdy, dressed in rustic fur coats. They had the weathered, lively faces typical of the poor, which clashed with the elegance of Ladbroke Square.

"Excuse me, sirs," I said, taking a deep breath. "Could I ask the name of the man who lives in this house?"

"Sure," one of the two men replied. "Mr. William Hallett lives here with his family. But now you've got to tell us . . . what's it to you?" he asked rudely.

"I absolutely must speak to Mr. Hallett!" I said

breathlessly. "It's of the utmost importance . . . a matter of life and death!"

The two looked at each other and burst out laughing. One pushed his fur coat aside, letting me see the pistol that was wedged in his belt, while the other began speaking again.

"Look, miss," he jeered. "My poor mummy always told me never to trust redheads, because they're liars! And I always follow my mummy's advice . . . so I suggest you make yourself scarce."

"You don't understand!" I replied. "This isn't a prank. Mr. Hallett really is in grave danger! If you'd just let me warn him —"

At that point, the thug with the pistol lost his patience, pulling it from his belt.

"Listen here, squirt!" he addressed me, waving his weapon in the air. "Tell us who sent you here with these gimmicks, you understand? No one gets through here, by order of Mr. Hallett. If you thought your pretty face and scatterbrained look would enchant us, well, you've made a big mistake!"

When he eventually pointed the pistol right at my face, I finally raised my hands in surrender.

"Okay, I'll leave . . . but you're the ones who

are making a big mistake!" I said weakly, my voice quivering with anger.

Lowering my head so I wouldn't have to see those two obnoxious characters, I walked past the building and continued until I was far from that corner of the square. As soon as I was out of sight of those two, however, I stopped and filled my lungs with the cold December air.

Today I smile when I think about it. But back then, my first thought went to the ruthless Hilda, whom I'd never seen but who I imagined — who knows why? — had a thick mane of blond curls and two proud, flashing eyes. What would Hilda have done in my place? She wouldn't have given up at the slightest difficulty, leaving the whole investigation at a standstill.

Then I began to wonder, why was Mr. Hallett protecting himself by having those two brutes at his door? Could he possibly have the building guarded regularly?

Considering the out-of-place appearance of the two guards, I thought it highly unlikely. Instead, those two seemed to be thugs from the slums who'd been hired hastily to meet an urgent need.

But if that was the case, things became even more mysterious: maybe Hallett already knew he was in danger! And if that was the case, how did he know? Had he figured out the fake chess problem that appeared in the *Times*, too? Had he discovered what might happen by reading about the murders of Peccary and Barrow in the papers? With a whirlwind of questions swirling in my head, I was itching to get to the bottom of the story.

So I can honestly say that what pushed me to act was true curiosity rather than a wish to imitate the mysterious Hilda.

I made up my mind: I would try to get close to the back of Hallett's house. So I ran until I reached the other side of the block and came out onto a wide street named Ladbroke Road.

What I saw discouraged me.

Several gardens belonging to the buildings on Ladbroke Square overlooked this street. If I could sneak into one of them, I would be able to sneak in the back of the building that was being watched by those two rude men. This proved impossible, however. Tall brick walls and strong, barbed fences protected the gardens.

Not even my acrobatic friend Lupin would be able to get past obstacles like these, I thought.

Still, I inspected the barriers, but I wasn't able to find even one small gap that would allow me to enter through the back garden. In the end, I had to give up on that attempt. But I wasn't going to give in completely just yet!

I continued to another block and turned onto the first street on the left. I walked until I had gone all the way around Ladbroke Square.

My plan was very simple — I wanted to get near the house without the two men seeing me, and then hide behind the park fence in order to spy on the entrance to Hallett's home. I wasn't expecting the two brutes to leave their posts, but I thought maybe one of them would go out on an errand. That way, I would be able to get closer and get a message to the owner of the house.

I was brooding over the details of my alternative plan when I saw something curious. In the exact place where I'd decided to hide in order to spy on the Hallett home, I noticed that the snow was trampled over, as if someone had been there, pacing back and forth, for a long time.

Is it possible that I am not the first person to hide in this corner of Ladbroke Square? I thought. *Who else would have hidden in that very corner where you could glimpse the entrance to Hallett's house, if not . . . the person who was after him?*

That thought made my heart jump into my throat. But I tried to stay as calm as I could, and I knelt to check the footprints in the snow. Unfortunately, whoever had hidden there before me had trampled the snow so thoroughly that no visible tracks remained.

As I stood back up, I noticed a piece of crumpled yellow paper at the bottom of the gate. I picked it up and examined it carefully. It was a small greeting card, and I could see traces of ink written on it.

The little piece of paper, however, had been creased and folded by someone's fingers so many times before being tossed to the ground that I couldn't read the print at all. I put it in my pocket, intending to give it to Sherlock.

A thousand more questions began chasing each other in my mind when I heard a sound behind me. I turned with a jerk.

I saw something.

But it was only for a fraction of a second. What I saw didn't last long enough for me to clearly remember it.

Then I felt a sharp jab right below the nape of my neck.

And everything went dark.

Chapter 11

A LONG, TROUBLED DREAM

Where had I wound up? What street in London was this, so long and narrow, with these two rows of short, dark little houses, without even one lit window?

The sky was an angry, shadowy gray, and the occasional streetlight gave off halos of ghostly greenish light. I quickened my steps, starting to run, but to my anguish, I found that no matter what road I took, that long, dark street continued to stretch out before me, no end in sight.

As if that discovery wasn't disturbing enough, when my glance fell upon the large stone slabs making up the sidewalk, I distinctly saw, in one corner, a small circle drawn in yellow chalk. It was identical to the one I had glimpsed in the places the mysterious Black Friar had picked for his murders.

My throat closed, making it hard to breathe. I looked around, feeling lost. I could only hear the wind whistling in this deserted place.

"Endless streets do not exist!" I told myself, trying to feel brave. And I started walking again as quickly as I could, my head bowed.

Suddenly, I saw another of those yellow circles come into view on the sidewalk, then another and yet another. It was as if an evil, invisible hand was drawing these cursed colored marks, anticipating my path.

I looked at them more closely and realized that the small circles were actually thin strings, which some awful enchantment was animating and making slither along the stones of the sidewalk. The anxiety I felt turned into real terror.

I tried to run, but the evil yellow threads covering the sidewalk were now clinging to my ankles, making me immobile.

I felt trapped and screamed . . .

★ ★ ★

I found myself surrounded by a soft, dim light. A few moments were all it took for me to realize I was stretched out in my bed. My forehead was sweaty, and my hands clung to the hem of a linen sheet. The long, dark street; the dusky streetlights; the evil threads that had trapped my feet . . . they had all vanished in an instant.

"Irene . . . Irene! You're awake!" said a trembling voice next to me.

I turned and saw my father, his face strained and his eyes shining. Behind him stood my mother, who sighed.

"My God, what a fright you've given us, my little one!" Papa said.

I wanted to get out of bed and hug Papa, but as soon as I moved, I felt a sharp pain in my neck and lay my head back on my pillow.

It was far from pleasant. But the jolt of pain at least cleared the fog that was clouding my mind, helping me wake up the rest of the way.

My father took my hand in his and kissed it. "Irene . . . my little one . . . what happened?!" he asked.

I was awake and completely alert, but I couldn't answer that simple question. At that moment, the only thing I was certain of was that I mustn't tell him what I'd been doing in Notting Hill the previous evening. I closed my eyes and coughed in order to use a little time. I was just opening my mouth, still unsure about what I could invent, when I heard Mr. Nelson's voice.

"If you'll allow me . . . perhaps Miss Irene is struggling to remember due to the blow to her head, but I was with her and can therefore tell you . . ."

"All right then, Mr. Nelson. Go ahead and speak!" my mother urged him curtly.

"Of course, Mrs. Adler," he began. "You see, yesterday afternoon, Miss Irene realized she had forgotten to buy a gift for her cousin, Miss Josephine, who will be coming to visit her right after Christmas. So she decided, understandably so, if I may add, to go to Portobello Road to take care of this oversight. As always, I accompanied Miss Irene, and so I was there to witness the regrettable accident she was met with."

I must confess that at first, Mr. Nelson's words left me bewildered. What was this complicated lie about a gift for my cousin Josephine, whose visit I had actually forgotten? I now realize how silly I was not to see the simple truth! Mr. Nelson was protecting me once again.

"Unfortunately," Mr. Nelson continued, "as Miss Irene was crossing the street, a coachman, whom I have reason to think was drunk, caused his horses to spook. Your daughter took fright, tripped, and hit her head when she fell, losing consciousness. And that's what happened, Mr. and Mrs. Adler."

"And you, Mr. Nelson? Great Scott, what were you doing? Is it not your job to protect my Irene?" My father's voice thundered through the room, startling me.

I knew Papa as a kind, good-natured person, and his burst of anger deeply moved me. I had only heard him speak like this once before: upon our arrival at the port of Dover a few months before, when my friend Sherlock Holmes had come up to me disguised as a beggar, and I, not recognizing him, had fallen to the ground in fright.

Mr. Nelson lowered his gaze. "You're right, Mr. Adler," he replied. "I should have been more attentive. I hope you can forgive me."

"My faith in you is shaken, Mr. Nelson," my father said. "I reserve the right to make whatever decision regarding you that seems suitable!"

These words were too much for me, and ignoring the pain I felt in my neck, I sat up in bed. "Papa, that's not fair!" I protested. "What happened isn't at all Mr. Nelson's fault! I was the one who . . . " I hesitated for a moment, thinking of what I could say, and then continued, ". . . crossed the street suddenly, without looking first, like a complete fool," I concluded.

Papa smiled at me, turning his familiar, gentle face toward me. "All right, my little one, all right . . ." he soothed me. "Don't get upset. The worst is over, and you must just focus on resting."

I nodded, putting my head back on my pillow. Just then, the doorbell rang. A few moments later, my mother came back into the room, accompanied by a pompous man with a bushy gray mustache.

It was our neighbor, Dr. Harrison. Everyone said he was a great inspiration. He had only agreed to come take a look at me out of respect for my father. He did a brief examination, ending by giving my parents the obvious advice that I should stay warm and rest completely.

The idea that I should rest in bed for who knows how long made me anxious. As soon as Dr. Harrison left, I asked for a cup of hot chamomile tea, so I could speak directly with Mr. Nelson.

When our butler came over to me carrying a cup of steaming tea, I put my hand on his arm. "Thank you, Mr. Nelson!" I whispered. "I'd be in a lot of trouble now without you."

Mr. Nelson nodded his head slightly and gave something halfway between a smile and a short sigh.

"You're kind, miss, but in truth, I don't think I've managed to put the slightest dent into your limitless talent for getting into trouble!" he said.

I smiled, too. "You're one of a kind, Mr. Nelson, and I don't know how I can ever repay you," I said, clasping his arm more firmly. "But now I'm terribly curious. You have to tell me what really happened yesterday evening!"

The butler looked around to make sure my parents weren't nearby, and then began softly. "It's simple. Yesterday afternoon, I was at the window when you came home, and I saw you conversing with your friend, Master Holmes. I know that always means there's trouble brewing and so, when I realized you had no intention of coming into the house, I followed you at a distance. I suppose you remember having walked to the square in Notting Hill, where a brute threatened you with a pistol?" Mr. Nelson asked.

I nodded.

"Right then," he continued, "I was about to come out and bring you home. But at that moment, you fled. I tried to follow you as you ran through the carriage traffic, but I lost track of you. Unfortunately, I only managed to find you once again when I heard you cry out. I rushed to you and found you collapsed on the ground by the fence in the park. There was no trace of the scoundrel who struck you, unfortunately."

I was absorbed in my thoughts for several moments. Hearing Mr. Nelson's tale brought back to mind all that had happened to me the day before at Ladbroke Square.

Or, more accurately, almost all.

Because in my memory, the last moments before being hit on the head and collapsing were surrounded by fog, like the details of a dream that is about to be forgotten.

I was sure something had happened . . . there was something I saw before darkness had descended on my mind. But no matter how hard I tried, I could not manage to grasp it.

I gave up with a sigh and took the cup that Mr. Nelson had brought me. I tried to set it on the nightstand, but the butler stared daggers at me, and I changed my mind.

After all he'd done for me, the least I could do was drink my tea!

* * *

I spent the following hours in the cocoon-like atmosphere of my room. Through a gap in the curtains, I could see that it had begun to snow again.

My head was filled with questions: where was Lupin? Would I see him again? And Sherlock? I wondered if he had been able to contact Mr. Hallett, the next intended victim.

I meant to ask Mr. Nelson to bring me the evening paper so I could find out if the triple homicide had been carried out, but before that could happen, I was lulled into a peaceful drowsiness by the slow descent of snowflakes.

A good amount of time passed like this, until I felt a gentle hand rest on my shoulder. It was my father, and at the door, standing as stiff as two boards, were Sherlock and Lupin.

It was obvious that they weren't used to official visits. Wearing formal expressions and holding their hats in their hands, they looked really comical.

"Your two friends have come to visit," said Papa, gesturing toward them. "I was sure you'd be happy to see them, so I let them in. But I also warned them that the doctor recommended absolute rest. So I cannot give you time for more than a brief hello . . . I'll be back in five minutes."

After patting my cheek, he excused himself and left my friends alone with me. Sherlock and Lupin, however, stayed standing at the door like statues. I looked at Lupin, questioning, and he knew what I was wondering right away.

"My father and I have agreed I'll rejoin him at Dunkirk at the start of the year. Before then, I can stay here in London," he said.

I smiled. That was really good news. But time was short, and the three of us were in the midst of an investigation.

"Come on!" I said, hurrying them on. "You heard we only have a little time, didn't you? Come here and tell me if there's any news about the Scarlet Rose affair."

Lupin jumped up and came over to lean against my bed. "You . . . you're okay, right? For a moment I was afraid that . . . " he said, ignoring my command to report on the investigation.

"Don't worry," I reassured him. "My neck just hurts a bit, but it will be better tomorrow. But how did you find out?"

"Mr. Nelson left us a message at the Shackleton Coffee House," Sherlock said, coming closer to my bed. "We came here as soon as we could. I don't think I need to tell you that going to Hallet's house and Ladbroke Square alone was a grave error that could have cost you very dearly!" he added in a serious voice.

"Oh, don't be dramatic, Holmes!" I said. "It was just a blow to the head, after all. Now let's get to the news."

Since neither of them said anything right away, I began by relaying my own findings.

"I will tell you what I discovered for the price of a

small bump on my neck," I said. "The third intended victim is named Hallett, but it seems that someone has already warned him. He has his house guarded by two armed men who won't let anyone get close. In addition —"

"In addition?" Sherlock asked.

"I also discovered that in a little corner, just outside the park in Ladbroke Square, someone was posted to spy on Hallett's home," I finished.

"That same 'someone' who hit you over the head, I suppose," said Lupin.

"And perhaps that same 'someone' who entertained himself by committing murders and thefts around the city, leaving behind a scarlet rose!" Sherlock added.

The thought that it could have been the killer who hit me on the head sent a shiver down my spine.

"Curses!" I swore through clenched teeth. "If only I could remember . . . "

"Sorry, remember what?" Sherlock asked, confused.

"What I saw before collapsing!" I said, frustrated. "I'm sure I saw something, but it's like my mind can't latch onto the memory."

"I think I read that's very common after a certain degree of trauma," Lupin said. "Maybe it's just a matter of time and then you'll be able to remember what you saw."

Sherlock nodded, fascinated. "The human mind is like a large labyrinth," he declared. "And perhaps right now, Irene, in some corner of your labyrinth roams the phantom of a killer."

Chapter 12

LIKE A TIGER IN A CAGE

It was very frustrating knowing that I had an important piece of truth in my head that I could not bring into focus. I grumbled, lying back on the pillows, and tried to think about something else.

By chance, my eyes fell on the dark heap of my bunched-up blue coat, which someone must have put on the back of the chair when I was brought to bed the day before. My gaze slipped over to the pockets, with their silvery velvet flaps, and it was then that I saw myself standing there, next to the Ladbroke Square fence, sliding something into my pocket.

"The slip of paper!" I exclaimed under my breath, drawing intrigued looks from Sherlock and Lupin. But there wasn't time for an explanation. "Check in the pockets of my coat," I told them.

Sherlock, who was closer, pulled the folded-up scrap of paper I had picked up the day before from my coat pocket. Then he stared at me, puzzled.

"I found it yesterday in the corner where the snow had been trampled," I explained, "where someone before me must have hidden to spy on Hallett's house."

Sherlock quickly sprang up and walked over to the lamp on my nightstand. "Traces of ink are still visible. Something was written . . . but the paper is all worn out, as if . . . " he trailed off.

"As if someone had turned it over and over in his hands," Lupin jumped in.

Sherlock straightened his back and stared into space. "Of course. Whoever was spying on Hallett's house was nervous," he said, trying to envision the scene. "He found that piece of paper in his pocket and began to roll it between his fingers, twisting and bending it until something caught his attention, and he let it fall to the ground . . . "

Just then there was a sound of footsteps on the stairs. Papa was coming, which meant our time was almost up.

"What are you going to do now?" I quickly asked.

"We'll go back to Mr. Field," Lupin answered. "He's just been released from jail."

"And considering how Inspector Babbington treated him, I suspect he'll want revenge!" Sherlock added.

I looked at the doorway of my room, thinking about how my friends would soon be gone, leaving me alone. I felt a pang in my heart, much stronger than the pain in my head.

"Sherlock, Arsène . . . I have to stay closed up in here, due to doctor's orders," I said. "But don't leave me out, all right?"

"Promise," Sherlock nodded.

"We never thought of leaving you out, Irene," said Lupin, smiling at me. "Take a look at the garden in the back every so often, okay?" he added with a wink.

I returned his smile and nodded my agreement to keep an eye out for his secret visits. But my smile was a sad one.

Papa had just appeared at the door, and as if enchanted by some strange magic, Sherlock and Lupin became as rigid as two statues again. They respectfully said goodbye to Papa and each took their leave of me with a bow.

I stayed alone in my room and let myself fall onto my pillows with a deep sigh. *Field was out of prison,* I thought. *And I? When would I be out of mine?*

I decided that in order to survive being cooped up, I would give myself a goal. I set my sights on doing everything I could to show my parents that I was calm and healthy. In this way, I hoped I could shorten the period of absolute rest that Dr. Harrison had prescribed for me to a day or a little more.

Sticking to my plan, when dinnertime arrived, I got out of bed, put on a satin bathrobe and slippers, and went downstairs.

My mother greeted me with a stern look to let me know that I shouldn't have gotten up. She told me that Mr. Nelson had been about to bring me dinner in bed on a tray.

"Mother, I don't actually feel weak, plus . . . don't you think the family cheer and the warmth of the crackling fire might help?" I asked, looking over at my father, who was sitting in an armchair smoking his pipe.

"Indeed, Genevieve, I think that . . . " Papa began.

I smiled. I knew I could always count on Papa's support! So the place settings were changed and dinner was served to everyone on a small table next to the glowing fireplace.

I did not have much of an appetite, but I pretended to enjoy my consommé and boiled chicken. After dinner, I happily accepted the tiny splash of port that Papa poured in my glass, commenting that it was a "cure-all for body and spirit." Then I managed to snatch a little more time chatting by the fireplace, with Papa telling funny stories about his trip to Glasgow. But after a half hour, my mother stood up and pointed toward the door.

"Enough stretching the rules . . . to bed!" she ordered me, just as she had when I was five years old. I pretended to collapse on the arm of the sofa, the victim of an angry fit. I earned a scolding from Mama and a hearty laugh from Papa.

In any case, that was all I could manage that evening. I lingered long enough to give my parents each a kiss. Then I went to my room, where I found comfort in my diary. Luckily I had much to write down.

When I finally put it away after recording the bits of information that seemed far from forming a clear picture (the Black Friar's code, the potential return of the Scarlet Rose Gang, the men guarding Hallett's home, the attack I had suffered . . .), I drifted back to sleep.

The next morning, I awoke while it was still dark outside. I looked at the clock in the corner of my room and discovered with shock that it was not yet seven!

An endless span of hours stretched ahead of me, promising eternal boredom. I turned on my desk lamp and added an entry to my diary. I read a story and looked at the time again — a little past eight! I wondered how time could pass so terribly slowly.

As I made myself breakfast, I waited for the arrival of the errand boy who delivered a bundle of newspapers for my father. I dove into the newly printed pages of the *Times*, looking feverishly for any mention of Ladbroke Square or Mr. Hallett . . . nothing.

I wondered if the third murder in this horrible

series had been committed and, if it had, if Scotland Yard had decided to keep the news under wraps. Sherlock and Lupin probably already had the answers to my questions.

It was then that I suddenly remembered Lupin's promise — to come update me on the news by sneaking into the back garden.

I began to roam around the house, like a spirit in purgatory, constantly returning to the small door that led to the garden to see if my friend had come.

As I finished my obsessive route once more and found myself — for the umpteenth time — passing the door to the small room where Mr. Nelson was busy polishing the silver, our butler didn't restrain himself any longer.

"Miss Adler!" he burst out. "Aren't you supposed to be observing absolute rest? You seem more like the Indian tiger that I saw shut up in a cage at the Great Circus of the Orient when I was a little boy!"

"The tiger is a noble, proud animal, so I'll take that as a compliment," I replied, peering into the room. "As for the fact that I feel as though I'm in a cage, dear Mr. Nelson, that's the pure and simple truth!"

Mr. Nelson muttered something I didn't hear as I began my round toward the garden again.

But I still did not see Lupin.

Instead, I heard noises from the floor above and realized my parents had awakened. So I ran to my room and buried myself back under the covers, ready for them to visit me.

That morning, I was lucky. Papa ate breakfast quickly and went to the city for some business, while my mother shut herself away sewing in a remote parlor, far from the stairs and the hallway leading to the back garden. That meant that, at least for a bit, I had a clear field for making my rounds!

Even my constant roaming, however, wound up boring me.

I was completely frustrated when, during my millionth trip through the main hallway of the house, I paused to look at the old family portraits hanging on the walls, yawning. Great-Great-Grandfather Wolfgang with his long white beard, Great-Grandfather Leopold with his solemn hooked nose, Great-Aunt Marguerite with her icy eyes . . .

It was right when I was staring at Great-Aunt Marguerite's forbidding portrait that something clicked in my mind. It almost felt like a gear that had been stuck for a long time had finally begun to work again.

My heart sped up. Once again, I looked over the details of the portrait: black dress, gnarled hands, starched collar, face covered with fine wrinkles and then . . . I had it!

I was so excited I had to take a small step back to lean against the wall.

It had happened! The memory that I'd thought was lost somewhere in the darkness of my mind had finally resurfaced. Now I was certain of what I had seen before I'd collapsed that day in Ladbroke Square!

I ran to the back door hoping to find Lupin so I could tell him what had just happened. But he still wasn't there.

I went back to look a few minutes later and by then was so used to circling in vain that I was about to close the door again when . . .

Was that a gray hat I saw popping over the garden wall? I went back to look and spotted Lupin, who was waving his hat in the air to get my attention.

"Lupin! Lupin!" I whispered, gesturing for him to

come closer. My friend leaped over the wall as easily as if he were opening a door and joined me.

"Hello, Irene!" he called.

"Hello, Arsène. You don't know how happy I am to see you . . . but we don't have much time. My mother could come by here any minute," I said hurriedly.

"I'll be quick as a flash! I promise," Lupin said. "First of all, you were right about Hallett's strange behavior. Mr. Field, who is now investigating on his own, tried meet with Hallett. He wanted to help him of course, but the guards shoved him out the door! Then there's Sherlock's new discovery. That lunatic spent the whole night examining the piece of paper you found in Ladbroke Square and figured out it was a ticket!"

"A ticket?" I asked.

"Yes, a train ticket. For the Liverpool-London line," Lupin told me.

My eyes widened. That unexpected detail made the whole story seem even more puzzling . . . but now it was my turn to speak. "Believe it or not, Arsène, I also have news."

"So what are you waiting for?" he asked.

"Remember when I told you I'd seen something before collapsing," I began, "but that I couldn't remember what it was anymore?"

"Don't tell me that —" Lupin started.

"Yes!" I interrupted. "I finally managed to remember . . . it was the eyes!"

"Eyes?!"

"Yes, Arsène, exactly that!" I said. "The eyes of a woman! Blue and as sharp as a blade of ice."

Chapter 13

A TRIP TO LIVERPOOL

Unfortunately, the events I'm about to relate to you did not take place before my eyes. Despite my attempts to appear cheerful and in perfect health, Dr. Harrison considered it inappropriate to shorten the length of the torture that kept me shut into our Aldford Street home while my friends were out on London's city streets hunting down a dangerous, nameless, faceless murderer.

The tale of what had happened during those days — which Lupin recounted to me later — was, however, so animated, fascinating, and richly detailed that thinking back on it today, I feel as if I had really been there the whole time. And here's how things went . . .

* * *

When I closed the little back door again, Lupin leaped over the garden wall and went to meet Sherlock. This time they were not meeting at the Shackleton Coffee House, but at Holmes's.

As Lupin got close to the Holmes residence, he saw a blackish column of smoke rising from the wooden toolshed in the garden and went there without hesitating.

The scene that met Lupin's eyes when he entered the shack was as chaotic as it was familiar: the peat stove rumbling furiously in the corner, Sherlock sunk in an old armchair, elbows propped on the armrests, fingertips together. His eyes were fixed on an unknown point outside the dusty window, while all around him there was a genuine apocalypse of newspapers, torn apart and scattered across the floor.

Sherlock stayed as still as a statue, without even greeting Lupin. Sighing, Lupin ventured on tiptoe into this jungle of ink and paper.

"*Liverpool Echo* . . . *Mersey Star* . . . *Northern Herald* . . .*" read Lupin, spotting here and there the names of the newspaper headers that Sherlock had torn apart. They were all daily papers from Liverpool and the surrounding areas. "Are you starting to be attracted to the rough charm of northern England?" Lupin joked.

Sherlock waved his hand in agitation, as if he were shooing a fly. "Liverpool . . ." he then said, speaking more to himself than to Lupin, who was now standing beside him. "The ticket Irene found in that hidden corner of Ladbroke Square tells us that Liverpool is one of the places this whole odd affair revolves around . . . but how? Darn it, how?! What exactly does Liverpool have to do with this?" he asked, furiously kicking a few sheets of paper that were under his feet.

Lupin made a face, which meant he hadn't the foggiest idea, picked up a wooden footstool, and straddled it directly in front of Sherlock. "The only thing I know about Liverpool is that an old friend of Papa's lives there — a soldier," Lupin said. "A guy named Pepper who sends funny postcards from time to time . . . but I'm afraid that won't help you at all."

"Brilliant conclusion, Arsène," Sherlock said, slowly leaning his head back. "But don't worry. You're in good company! Even this heap of Liverpool newspapers that I asked Sparky to find for me wasn't any use! Just a confused jumble of facts and insignificant events . . . not a single tile that can fit into our puzzle of Black Friars and scarlet roses," he said, irritated.

"I'm afraid this may be what we French call a *cul de sac* — a dead end," Lupin said. "But there's at least some news! Irene has remembered what she saw before being knocked out in front of the Hallett mansion."

Sherlock looked over at Lupin listlessly. He lowered his chin slightly, which indicated he wasn't expecting much of the news Lupin was about to share.

"Sharp, blue eyes . . . a woman's eyes, according to Irene," Lupin revealed.

At first Sherlock was uninterested in this detail, which seemed vague to him and of little promise. He stroked his chin, puzzled.

Lupin, on the other hand, was just about to suggest a snack at the pub on the street corner when Sherlock suddenly jumped to his feet. Lupin swears he saw our friend change from one second to the next, much like a werewolf when a full moon appears.

Sherlock threw himself onto the ground, actually plunging into the piles of newspaper scattered across the floor. He began to examine them feverishly, his eyes flickering anxiously as he skimmed through the columns, throwing the pages into the air when he didn't find what he was looking for.

"For heaven's sake, would you mind telling me what the devil —" Lupin said in disbelief, getting up from his stool to avoid being hit in the face by the newspapers Sherlock was tossing.

"A woman . . . a woman . . . a woman . . . a woman . . ." Sherlock repeated, throwing the papers.

Just as Lupin was becoming afraid he was witnessing our friend's final decline into madness, Sherlock grabbed a sheet of paper with both his hands and stood up. "Here it is! Finally!" he exclaimed triumphantly, showing the page to Lupin, his finger pointing to a tiny news blurb in the *Liverpool Echo*.

"Young woman vanishes from Liverpool," Lupin began reading. "Mrs. Mary Musgrave, married, with two sons, residing with her family at number eighty-eight Duke Street. The woman's sudden disappearance occurred this morning. The woman's husband, Mr. Adrian Musgrave, who reported her missing to the police, stated that some clothing and a small suitcase were missing from the woman's closet. Therefore, the most believable theory is that she has fled. According to unconfirmed reports from police, a person with features similar to those of Mary Musgrave was sighted early in the morning at the Lime Street railway station platforms. The reasons for her disappearance at this point remain unknown and —" Lupin broke off and looked at Sherlock with wide eyes. "And what do we think happened to this nice lady?"

"Look at the date of the paper!" Sherlock shouted at him. "December thirteenth. Tuesday! The day after the Black Friar's classified ad was published! The day of the first murder in Twickenham! A woman. And it was the eyes of a woman that Irene says she saw before collapsing. A woman traveled by train from Liverpool, most probably toward London, and perhaps with the very same ticket that's now sitting on my nightstand!"

Lupin stopped in the middle of the room with his hands on his hips, considering Sherlock's imaginative theory. Then he shook his head. "Have you ever heard of a coincidence? You're getting so excited over things that could simply be common coincidences, my friend!" he said.

Sherlock reacted with a sneering laugh. "Coincidence? Do you know what coincidences are?" he asked. "They're excuses made by those with lazy minds in order to avoid having to discover the truth!"

Lupin shrugged, defeated. He knew well that when Sherlock was this firmly convinced, not even a gunshot could dissuade him from what he had in mind. "All right," Lupin said. "So what are you thinking of doing?"

"Going to check to make sure my little sister has fully recovered. She seemed better when she awoke," Sherlock answered, suddenly in a marvelous mood.

"What? Why?!"

"Because tomorrow morning we must be free of commitments," Sherlock explained. "There's a train for Liverpool that leaves from Euston Station at seven on the dot!"

★ ★ ★

And so the following day at dawn, my friends found themselves under the grand arch of Euston Station. Lupin, a bitter enemy of early awakenings, was yawning and gasping like a fish out of water, while Sherlock, alert and quick off the mark, didn't even seem to know what time of day it was.

The journey to Liverpool passed in perfect silence. Sherlock was deep in thought, watching the snow-covered countryside pass by the window, while Lupin dozed off. After about four hours, the train stopped chugging at the crowded Lime Street Station.

It wasn't until Lupin got off the train, the brisk December air sweeping across his face, that he realized he didn't know an important detail. "So . . . where exactly are we going?" he asked.

"The Office of Vital Statistics. This way!" Sherlock said.

Sherlock had studied the map of Liverpool the night before and moved confidently through the city although he was visiting for the first time. The Office of Vital Statistics proved to be a forgettable, gloomy building. It stood near the harbor area and looked out onto the River Mersey.

Sherlock and Lupin arrogantly pushed through the door and found themselves in front of a desk manned by a portly official who was reading the paper. "Sir?" Sherlock addressed him firmly. "My friend and I need to consult your records."

The large man looked up from the paper and studied them carefully. Sherlock's speech, completely lacking the rough northern accent, must have made the man think that the two young men in front of him were upper-class children, brought up in Cambridge or Oxford.

"Well, I'll be . . ." the man snapped. "Don't you high-class kids have anything better to do than to come play at the Office of Vital Statistics? What kind of a world are we living in?"

"Sir, you are doubly in error," Sherlock replied, stung. "First of all, my friend and I are far from being from upper-class families, and second, we haven't come here to play but to carry out research that could save a life!"

The portly official's first response was merely a grunt. "Sorry, lads," he finally said. "You'll have to save the world another day. Regulations restrict you from consulting the archives in the Office of Vital

Statistics unless you're adults and have brought a formal written request."

Sherlock shook his head, bit his lip, and sighed. Lupin, who had expected an explosion of anger, was very surprised to see his friend back down gracefully and exit the building without saying a word.

"Four hours by train and we give up like that?" Lupin asked in disbelief.

"Don't be absurd, Arsène. Obviously we're not giving up. It's proper to try doing things the right way first, but now we're justified in moving onto more . . . adventurous methods!" Sherlock answered.

"Great! And do you have a particular method in mind?" Lupin asked.

"Yes," Sherlock confirmed. "You will create a diversion, which will allow me to get into the archives." He looked at Lupin with a challenging air of amusement.

I suspect anyone else in a similar situation would have told Sherlock to get lost, but Lupin didn't. Instead, he looked back at him and smiled, saying, "Wait for me here. This could take a few minutes."

With those words, Lupin walked to the back of the building. He found an open door where a maid was cleaning the floor. That was all it took for Lupin to come up with a plan. Moving as quietly and deftly as a cat, he stole a bucket of rags from the maid and sneakily headed for the basement. Once there, he found a concealed corner and, using the matches he always carried with him, set fire to the rags. Since they were damp, they gave off a column of whitish smoke — exactly as Lupin had hoped.

Within a couple of minutes, smoke was spiraling out from the basement door.

At that point, all that was left for Lupin to do was shout, "Fire! Fire!" and then run for it. While people in the building started to run in all directions, spreading the alarm, Sherlock spotted his friend leaving the building, coughing from the smoke he had inhaled.

"Come on!" Lupin shouted, coughing between words. "We should have at least ten minutes!"

Without another word, Sherlock followed Lupin to a different entrance, and as everyone else ran out, my two friends ran into the smoky building.

Chapter 14

PAPER LABYRINTH

Between the fire and the general uproar, no one noticed when my two friends snuck into the archives. Sherlock and Lupin hurriedly shut the door behind them and found themselves in a room with a very high ceiling. The walls were completely covered with wooden shelves on which sat forbidding volumes with black leather spines and gold writing. Sherlock ran to the middle of the room and began looking all over, nervously turning in circles. With his coat twirling around, he looked like a whirling dervish.

Suddenly, his eyes lit up, and he ran to a tall

wooden ladder that was used for reaching the top shelves.

Lupin watched our friend climb halfway to the top and examine several volumes before grabbing one. Sherlock flipped through it frantically, as if the pages were red-hot. When he finally stopped, a huge smile spread across his face. "Eureka!" he exclaimed, looking down at Lupin.

Just then, the man who had turned them away earlier barged into the room with a colleague. Apparently, they had discovered the bucket of burning rags.

"Scoundrels! Get away from those records!" the man shrieked.

Lupin looked around. The situation wasn't promising. He quickly took measure of the large room. "Climb! Climb to the top," he ordered as he hurriedly joined Sherlock on the ladder.

Sherlock hesitated for an instant but then did what Lupin said, protesting as he climbed. "Do you want to perch on top of the ladder the whole day?"

Lupin didn't answer and simply gestured to keep climbing.

"Now what?!" Sherlock asked when he reached

the top of the ladder, his head almost touching the ceiling. Arsène was right behind him.

"Now hold on tight, and when I say 'jump,' you jump. Got it?" Lupin asked. A moment later, Lupin leaned both hands against a shelf and vigorously pushed off, sending the both the ladder and the two of them into the air. Like the swing of a gigantic pendulum, the ladder moved in a wide arc under the ceiling of the room, rapidly plunging toward the opposite side of the archives.

"Now!" Lupin shouted right before the ladder crashed to the ground. He and Sherlock jumped off, tumbling onto a table against the wall. Next to it was a narrow hallway that led to a door, which Sherlock and Lupin ran through without a second thought.

"Stop! Scoundrels!" The official's loud voice rang out beneath the archive vaults. My friends declined his invitation to stop, however, and instead ran even faster.

The door led to another, bigger corridor, in which the smoke from the basement still lingered. Sherlock and Lupin crossed it, found the entrance, and exited, running until they reached a large, busy street, where they disappeared into the crowd.

About twenty minutes later, my friends were in a comfortable compartment on a train headed for London, which departed promptly at 1:13 p.m. With no other passengers near them, they were able to speak freely.

"Well," said Lupin as the train left the Liverpool station, "would you be so kind as to tell me why we just risked being detained at Her Majesty's pleasure?"

Sherlock curled his lips into a mysterious little smile and was silent, which exasperated Lupin, but likely made the situation all the more entertaining for Sherlock.

"One name: Mary Harding," he finally said, as Lupin rolled his eyes impatiently. "The maiden name of Musgrave's wife who ran away. Mary Harding, born in London on March 4, 1843."

Lupin didn't seem particularly impressed by that answer. "What use is that to us?" he asked, stretching his back.

"To know what we're going to do tomorrow, my dear Arsène," Sherlock answered.

"And what's that?" Lupin asked.

"Visit another Office of Vital Statistics!"

* * *

According to Lupin, the next morning it took them at least three hours to get ready. Three hours and a good deal of messing around with wigs, fake beards, moldable wax, powder, cotton balls, and other strange accessories that were part of the new disguise kit Sherlock had bought, sacrificing a good part of the money he'd earned writing riddles for the *Globe*. At the end of this lengthy procedure, however, my friends looked at themselves in a mirror and could barely recognize their own faces. Lupin was now a hairy character with a bushy brown beard, and Sherlock was a refined gentleman with gray hair; two thick, well-groomed whiskers going down his cheeks; and a monocle with a light-blue lens framing his left eye. Some old clothes Sherlock had snatched from trunks in his attic and two majestic black felt top hats capped their disguises.

As can be readily imagined when dealing with any of Sherlock's ideas, these disguises had been planned to the tiniest detail. Even their voices had to be adjusted to fit their characters. For this purpose, Sherlock prepared a foul, greenish-colored mixture that he forced Lupin to gargle. Lupin didn't dare ask what ingredients were in the vile concoction, and Sherlock was merciful enough not to reveal it to him.

The results were remarkable: my two friends' throats were burning, but their voices were audibly hoarse, which made them sound more like adults.

At that point, they only had to leave the tiny shed in Holmes's garden and go to the nearest square to test their disguises.

* * *

"Good day, sirs!" a coachman greeted them, opening the door to the carriage with a much deeper bow than that which my friends were accustomed to.

"Good day, good day," Sherlock mumbled gruffly. "To the Office of Vital Statistics on Caxton Street! Quickly, we're in a hurry."

"Right away, sirs!" the coachman said as he sprang into the driver's seat and cracked the whip. Sherlock and Lupin looked at each other, satisfied with the effect their stiff personalities seemed to be having.

"Things seem to be working perfectly, my dear Lazarus!" said Sherlock.

"I really can't deny that, my dear Phineas!" Lupin replied.

Those were the names my friends had chosen for their two bizarre characters: Lazarus Ulpin and Phineas Sholme, lawyers by profession.

By the time they entered the doorway to the central London Office of Vital Statistics on Caxton Street, Sherlock and Lupin were completely immersed in their roles. By a lucky coincidence, when they went to make their request, the official appeared to be new to the job.

"Hello there, young man! We're Ulpin and Sholme, lawyers. We have a task of utmost importance to deal with," Sherlock said. "Can we trust you?"

The scrawny young clerk looked at them with timid, watery eyes. "Of c-course, sirs," he replied. "How may I help you?"

"Ah! By performing a simple constabulary cross-reference check for me," Sherlock lied.

"C-c-constabulary cross-reference check . . . " repeated the clerk, swallowing hard.

"I swear! The younger generation . . . tsk!" Lupin complained, crossing his arms over his chest.

"Would the gentle sirs like me to consult a more experienced colleague?" the young man suggested, hurt.

"Why make a bad impression on your superiors, young man? Think of your career!" Sherlock bore down on him. "Take us with you to the archives, and then old Ulpin and Sholme will manage on our own. You'll always have time to learn what a constabulary cross-reference check is."

"Of course," Lupin agreed. "A fine young man like you will soon figure it out."

The poor young official turned red, and with a gesture of his hand, invited my friends to walk into a long, shadowy hallway. In the middle of the corridor, the three stopped in front of a wide door. The young file clerk took a key from his jacket pocket and unlocked the door, then opened it.

On the other side of the door was a huge, dimly lit area that had many dusty shelves filled with records that held secrets of generation after generation of Londoners. The history of countless lives entrusted to a grand labyrinth of paper and ink!

Sherlock barely had time to grasp the exciting vastness of that thought. With a deep sigh, he returned to the role of the eccentric lawyer Sholme. "Can you lead us to the birth records for the year 1843, young man?" he asked.

"Of course," the clerk hastened to reply, wanting to look good. He led Sherlock and Lupin to a bookcase containing all the birth records for that year and stepped aside.

Upon seeing the huge tome in which the births of the first three months of 1843 were recorded, Sherlock attacked it like a starving animal. Skimming through the volume anxiously, he finally reached the pages for March fourth.

He rapidly scanned the names of everyone born that day, looking for the name Mary Harding.

But it was not there. "How the devil is that possible?" he muttered.

Lupin saw Sherlock scan those neat rows of ink again and again with increasing recklessness and frustration until . . .

The finger that was skimming along the page suddenly stopped. Sherlock's face froze, and his eyes shimmered violently.

"So is it there or not?" Lupin asked impatiently.

"No. There's no Mary Harding, but . . . " Sherlock trailed off.

"But?!" Lupin pressed.

"But there is a Mary Smeaton!"

Chapter 15

A TANGLED TALE

When I had recovered and was finally allowed to leave the house, I went to the Shackleton Coffee House at the hour of my typical meeting with Sherlock. I found my friend in his usual place, but today his face was radiant.

"Welcome back, Irene!" Sherlock greeted me, offering me a seat. "You came at just the right moment!"

"Is the Christmas spirit sneaking its way into your heart of stone, Sherlock?" I asked, walking over to the table.

"Not on your life!" Sherlock replied. "But yesterday was truly a successful day."

"Why is that?" I asked.

"Let's just say that two of our friends — two irritable lawyers — made a fantastic contribution to our investigation," Sherlock said.

"Could you be less vague?" I asked, looking at him as if he was speaking Arabic.

"A good deal of news surfaced at the London Office of Vital Statistics, Irene. We discovered that Gerald Smeaton, leader of the gang, was married to a woman with whom he had two children: Mary, the oldest, and Adam, whom Gerald's wife died giving birth to," Sherlock told me. "But the most unbelievable thing we discovered is that Mary Smeaton is probably involved in the matter we're investigating!"

"What?" I exclaimed. "The gang leader's daughter?"

"Precisely," Sherlock said. "Mary Smeaton, who was adopted along with her brother, Adam, changed her last name to Harding after the death of her father. Mary is now married, and she lives in Liverpool. I have reason to believe she fled her home and came to

London on the thirteenth of December!" With those words, Sherlock whipped around in his chair.

"Liverpool?" I repeated. "But then — "

"Yes," Sherlock cut me off. "The woman who assaulted you in Ladbroke Square may have been Mary."

I was still stunned by this incredible news when Lupin entered the café.

Lupin was in an excellent mood. As soon as he came in, he darted over to me and took my hand, squeezing it hard. "How nice to see you out of your prison!" he said, laughing. I laughed with him and confirmed that it was a huge relief to be able to poke my nose outside again.

"Did Sherlock give you the big news already?" he asked.

I nodded.

"Great! So what do you think of a little . . . demonstration?" Lupin asked, looking first at me and then at Sherlock.

Sherlock and I both stared at him, taken aback. "Demonstration?" we echoed together.

As his only answer, Lupin pulled a piece of paper from a leather bag he had under his arm and pinned it onto the threadbare upholstery of a nearby chair. Then he dropped into a different worn-out chair and pointed to the paper with a colored pencil.

"I shall now show you what happened," Lupin announced. He then drew a rose in the middle of the paper. "Now, this is the starting point." He drew two arrows and wrote "Police confidentiality" at the end of one and "Treason to the Crown" after the other.

"These are the two things we need to keep in mind," he continued. "That is, that the police requested that no journalist would write about the Scarlet Rose Gang, which the press agreed to. According to what Sparky reported, breaking the silence in the press would be punished as treason to the Crown. Why, do you suppose?"

Sherlock did not respond, and so I did. "Perhaps due to the wave of panic it created twenty years ago," I said.

Lupin made a face. "And do you think that's enough?" he asked skeptically.

"It depends who gave the order," Sherlock said.

"It depends on the reason the order was given," Lupin responded. Then he wrote "Jarvis" on the paper. "Do you remember him?" he asked.

I nodded. How could I have forgotten that delusional old policeman who was convinced there existed an obscure plot to assassinate the queen?

"What if Jarvis was right, in his own way?" Lupin asked.

Sherlock clasped his fingers under his chin and narrowed his eyes, beginning to reflect on it feverishly. "Continue," he said.

Lupin turned his back to us and continued to sketch out his diagram. "Here are some clues that led me to this conclusion. Elements that don't appear in the right place, assuming they have a right place."

Lupin wrote "Members of the original gang" and drew some arrows coming out from it. At the end of each arrow, he put a question mark, except for the last one, after which he wrote "Gerald Smeaton."

"So, this is the only name we have of an original gang member," Lupin said. "And what do we know for sure about him?"

"That he's dead," Sherlock said.

Lupin drew two arrows from Smeaton's name. "Not just that," he added. "We know he had a wife who died giving birth to their second child, and so today, there are . . ."

Lupin wrote two names: "Adam and Mary." And he underlined them.

"Smeaton died twenty years ago," Lupin continued. "And today, Gerald's children would be twenty-seven and twenty-five years old, respectively. We know that after the death of their father, the Harding family adopted the two children. Mary later moved to Liverpool and married Musgrave, but there's no trace of Adam."

After each name, Lupin drew a line on his diagram, which was beginning to spread out across the paper like a spiderweb. "However, we know that Smeaton's property was seized, and his two children were adopted by a family of modest means, so they certainly did not benefit from their father's loot."

"I read that Smeaton's possessions were few in number, but the gang surely collected a good deal of loot that wasn't found in the toolshed on the Thames," Sherlock said. "It seems likely that the other gang members divided the collection without him." He pointed to the other arrows.

Lupin shook his head. "Right — the others. In other words, this cloud of question marks," he said, gesturing to the question marks on the sheet of paper. "Who were the other members of the Scarlet Rose Gang?" Lupin asked. "We don't know for sure, but I believe that at least one of them must be a member of the top brass in the police force or part of the small group of people with access to the queen's palace."

Sherlock's eyes bulged. "What makes you say that?"

"The orders not to talk. 'Treason to the Crown.' Plus, don't forget what happened twenty years ago," Lupin said. "The police ignored all clues that had to do with the Scarlet Rose Gang, only to follow the hint that led to Smeaton all of a sudden. Why?"

"A stroke of luck after so many years wasted pursuing him with no results?" I offered.

"No, he was framed — a scapegoat — so that they could retire the investigation into the gang for good," Lupin said.

"Except it seems to have returned," I said.

And Lupin, quick as a fox, pointed his pencil to the names Adam and Mary. "But this isn't the original one. It's a new Scarlet Rose Gang. And I think that someone very important belongs to it, or perhaps, given that they would now be old, their children do."

Lupin looked at us and continued, "The train ticket . . . the woman Irene saw near Hallett's home, who could have been Mary. Don't you see? The Smeaton children have assumed their father's profession and are returning to challenge Scotland Yard!"

"Children who are even angrier than their parents were, it seems," I said. "As far as I know, the members of the original Scarlet Rose Gang didn't murder the victims of their robberies."

"That's precisely what doesn't add up!" Sherlock burst out. "Aside from the suggestion that someone in the palace or the police is involved, which is troubling to say the least."

"Babbington?" I suggested.

"No, he's too young," Sherlock said.

"But Babbington could be the son of one of the original members of the Scarlet Rose Gang!" Lupin said.

"The fact is, Arsène, that even if it were so, you haven't figured out the role Smeaton's children play in this," Sherlock replied.

Arsène sat down on the arm of a chair. "What do you mean?" he asked.

"If things are as you say — that twenty years after the crimes of the original gang, their heirs have swung back into action — why would they have included the children of Smeaton, the one member who was caught?" Sherlock asked.

"To make up for what happened?" I suggested.

"Then why didn't they help the Smeaton children out earlier?" Sherlock replied.

"Wait a second. Who said the Smeatons had been included?" Lupin said, smiling.

He drew one last arrow on the diagram, which went from Adam and Mary Smeaton to the Black Friar, and then he put a small circle around this last name.

"I don't understand," I muttered.

"My theory is that Smeaton's children were aware that the Scarlet Rose Gang was re-forming. I think they invented the Black Friar to let the other heirs know they were here, too. They used the Black Friar to warn them that they could somehow predict the gang's moves," Lupin explained.

"Interesting," I said. "But how did the Smeatons come to know about the others?"

"That's exactly what we have to find out," Lupin

said. He wrote "Harding," followed by a big question mark.

"Right!" I exclaimed. "What do we know about this Harding?"

"Nothing for now," Sherlock answered. "And it'll be difficult to learn anything more, since it's such a common last name."

"And about Musgrave?" I asked. "Perhaps he could be the link we're missing."

"We only have an address we can write to . . . unless you want to take another trip to Liverpool," Sherlock replied, pulling a crumpled piece of paper out of his pocket.

"If I were to bet," I stepped in, "I'd say that theirs was not a very happy marriage."

"That might be worth investigating," Lupin added.

"And Jarvis? Where does he fit into this whole reconstruction?" I asked.

Lupin answered that he believed someone from the police force was in the original gang and that Jarvis had probably discovered him.

"And that made him become insane?" I asked, skeptical.

Lupin himself had to admit it wasn't a good enough explanation.

With each new theory we devised, Sherlock grew increasingly annoyed — almost angry. "These two murders were accompanied by the theft of priceless personal objects, it's true," he muttered at one point. "But the thefts aren't at all comparable to the gang's spoils from before. The original Scarlet Rose Gang cleaned out entire jewelry stores. Banks. They emptied mansions of everything in a single night, whereas these thieves, in comparison, seem like amateurs."

"Children don't always surpass their fathers," Lupin muttered. "Particularly if they choose to challenge them in the same field."

"In addition," continued the young Holmes, ignoring him, "didn't you notice the strange similarity between the victims? They're all men in their fifties, rich but with humble origins, now living reclusive lives."

"It's no crime to put away money when you're young, nor to want to enjoy it in peace in your old age," Lupin replied.

Sherlock made another face, but this time he gave

Lupin the benefit of the doubt. "What if, instead of a new gang," he muttered, "it's exactly the same one as before, and the members decided to settle the score with the past?"

The mention of the past made me remember to check the time. I turned white. "Heavens! It's very late! I have to go home right now."

Sherlock, who was already on his feet, grabbed his coat as if he'd been waiting for an excuse to leave. "I'll come with you," he said.

Lupin slid back in his seat. "Are you saying you didn't like my idea?" he asked.

Sherlock fastened the buttons of his coat, and I noticed one was missing. "Not at all, Arsène, not at all," he replied. "It's really a good idea. But . . . something's missing. Or maybe it has something in it that's too . . . mad for my taste."

"He who lives without folly isn't so wise as he thinks," retorted Lupin, throwing his pencil onto the table. "François de La Rochefoucauld, French author."

Opening the door to the Shackleton Coffee House for me, Sherlock quoted in response, "If others had not been foolish, we should be so."

Arsène Lupin raised an eyebrow, questioning.

"William Blake," Sherlock Holmes said. "English poet."

Chapter 16

THREE GENTLEMEN, OR PERHAPS NOT

Sherlock Holmes walked next to me, his large hands buried in the pockets of his long green coat. Night was falling, and snowflakes drifted down on us from the dark, stone-colored sky.

Sherlock had offered to accompany me home, but neither of us was particularly in the mood for chatting after all the conversation we'd had that afternoon. I enjoyed his reassuring presence, however, and the sound of my shoes crunching against the snow.

Stopping by the window of a hat shop, we

lingered for a bit. Inside, the sales clerk was hurrying to pack up the final items from the wooden display heads for the evening. When he noticed us standing outside the window, he smiled at us. We smiled back. He held a funny checkered hat — a style my friend would become famous for in the future — out toward me, pointing at Sherlock.

"For Christmas?" I asked. "It's a good idea!"

I was obviously joking, but Sherlock, blushing from even the idea that I would buy him a present, said he didn't want any kind of hat. He gently pushed me away from the window, more embarrassed than ever.

We turned the corner, and I raised the collar of my overcoat to protect myself from the cold wind.

"You don't believe Lupin's theory, do you?" I asked my friend.

"I would say no," he replied, after several steps.

Above us, the smoke rose from the chimney stacks in black spirals and the clouds hid the stars.

Sherlock Holmes, whose brilliant mind could find logic in every event, accompanied me distantly, wrapped up in his somber thoughts. And I, who understood him so well, knew what he was thinking.

"Something doesn't make sense, right?" I asked.

"Something doesn't make sense," he confirmed.

While I paused, waiting on the sidewalk for him to decide to cross the last stretch of the street, I did a half pirouette, letting the snow land on my face. It was crisp and prickly on my lips.

"What doesn't make sense is Smeaton," Sherlock then said.

"What about Smeaton?" I asked.

Sherlock rubbed his temple. He wasn't wearing gloves, and his fingers had turned red from the cold. "How the police found him. Arsène is right to say that it's much too . . . fishy," he said.

"You're talking about the anonymous letter?" I asked.

He stared at me, as if surprised that I could reason as quickly as he. "Precisely," he responded.

We were facing each other in the snow, oblivious to anything else, including the front door of my house across the street. "That anonymous letter, which the police suddenly believed, led them to Smeaton's loot, and to his business card in plain sight." He spread out his arms in exasperation. "What robber goes around with a business card?"

I smiled at him. When he was thinking, the lines on his face relaxed and took on a solemn, ancient look, like some of the statues I had seen at the Louvre.

"Do you think Smeaton was set up?" I asked.

"Yes," he said, sighing and letting his arms go slack.

"By whom?"

Sherlock shook his head and said, "The only people who could have set him up had to have been those who knew the gang's plans."

"Perhaps it was that sleuth inside Scotland Yard?" I asked.

He stared at me. "In what sense?"

"Someone who pretended to receive an anonymous letter, arrange the search, and arrest Smeaton. Not that he was really the leader of the Scarlet Rose Gang," I said.

"Yes . . . he was only a small fish," Sherlock muttered. "And that way, all the others were let off the hook."

"They probably spent a good part of their haul, cleared their consciences, and slowly forgot about the past," I added.

Sherlock smiled. "And perhaps they became rich strangers in their fifties, who lived in lovely homes in elegant parts of the city . . . "

I grabbed his arm and exclaimed, "It was them! They were part of the Scarlet Rose Gang! Samuel Peccary, Joseph Barrow, and, therefore, also . . . Hallett?"

I stood on my tiptoes without even realizing it. When I stopped speaking, I found myself staring into the fiery eyes of Sherlock Holmes, clutching his arm in excitement.

When I realized what I was doing, I loosened my grip and dropped my heels back onto the snowy ground.

But I didn't stop looking at him.

"Just so," he responded, and I realized from the tone of his voice that his throat was dry, as if he'd just returned from a thought that had taken him far away. "They could be the old Scarlet Rose Gang traitors, whom the Black Friar has decided to punish after so many years."

I nodded. *Yes, that was possible,* I thought, but actually, I was dismayed.

There was some distraction that had come

between us — one that had nothing to do with our investigation but with the way that Sherlock and I were looking at each other.

I turned toward the front door of the house and said in a whisper, "Okay, Sherlock. We'll talk about it tomorrow. I'm going up."

I looked at him in the feeble light that came from the first floor and the row of the bright globes of streetlights, which looked like magic trees in a forest of stone.

I took a few steps, starting to cross the road.

"Irene?"

I stopped. "Yes?"

Sherlock then said something in a very soft, low voice, something that the whistling of the snowflake-filled wind kept from my ears. Perhaps it was something that had to do with his family, but I couldn't really hear it. I turned around, and when I saw him, chilled in the falling snow, it reminded me of Violet.

"And your sister?" I asked. "How is she? Has her fever gone down?"

Sherlock coughed. "Yes, of course. Yes, she's better. Much better."

I smiled and said, "I'm glad. Give her my best wishes, then. And now you try not to get sick, too."

"Of course," he repeated quietly. "Thank you."

And then with a leap, Sherlock Holmes caught up with me and hugged me so hard it left me breathless. I felt his face next to mine, his chin on my shoulder, his hands clasped behind my back.

Then right afterward, without saying a single word, he turned and walked away, disappearing into the snow.

Chapter 17

HUNTING THE BLACK FRIAR

As I walked down the steps in Miss Langtry's house the next day after my music lesson, I spotted Lupin crouching at the bottom of the stairway that led to the front door.

I dashed down the steps, excited, my fingers skimming the banister. When I started down the final flight though, I pretended to be surprised.

"So should I assume I'm being followed?" I asked, joining him in the entryway.

Lupin had changed his clothes and was wearing a dark brown overcoat with an elegant silk trim. I couldn't help but notice, and I complimented him on it.

"Things are going better with Papa," he said mysteriously.

"I'm glad," I said, smiling at him.

I arrived at the front door and went to open it, but Lupin prevented me from doing so, waving a copy of the *Times* in front of my face.

"What's happened?" I asked, alarmed. "Is it Hallett?"

"No, not that," he replied.

"For heaven's sake, Arsène!" I said. "Don't keep me hanging like this!"

He leaned against the front door like a real hooligan, flipping the pages of the *Times* under my nose. When he reached the classified pages, he showed me the most recent chess problem. It was followed by a sequence of letters, under which was written, "Check to queen early in the morning," and it was signed, "The White Friar."

It took me less than a second to figure out what had happened.

"Sherlock?" I whispered.

"So it seems," he replied.

"And what does he plan to do with this . . . bright idea?"

"It seems that yesterday evening, our friend found a way to speak to Hallett," Lupin explained.

My eyes widened. "How did he do it?"

"Don't ask me," he replied. "With all the surveillance that was around that house, not even my father could have managed to sneak in."

"Don't joke," I scolded him. It made me feel bad whenever Lupin insulted his father, even if it was done with humor.

"Anyway, I still don't have an answer. One of his disguises, I suppose," he said, starting to laugh.

I smiled, too, but I was perplexed.

"Getting Hallett to see him is a real success, but I really don't understand what it has to do with what he put in the *Times*," I said.

Lupin shrugged. "The thing is, Sherlock is in one of his moods," he explained.

This time I laughed heartily. I was possibly the only person in the world, besides Lupin of course, who could understand what this meant.

"Haunted looks and obscure riddles instead of normal sentences?" I asked.

"Exactly!" Lupin said, amused. "And you know how difficult it is to understand something when he's like that. Here's all I know: Sherlock left Hallett's house positive the chap wasn't telling the whole story about his past. In other words, that Hallet's not who he says he is."

"Oh," I said, trying to imagine what that fact could mean.

"And apparently this confirms a theory Sherlock came up with," Lupin continued. "About which, unfortunately, I'm in the dark and don't —"

I raised my hand to interrupt him so I could concentrate.

I remembered what Sherlock and I had talked about the day before in front of my house . . . the theory that the Black Friar's designated victims were Smeaton's old partners, who had betrayed him by setting him up with the anonymous letter.

Sherlock must have discovered that Hallett wasn't actually a tranquil, wealthy citizen, but a murky nouveau riche who was in cahoots with a bad crowd.

"Of course!" I exclaimed.

I excitedly explained to Lupin the theories that Sherlock and I had come up with on our walk home the day before and how Hallett's lies could fit into that puzzle.

"Now it all makes more sense," Lupin responded. "Even what seemed like sheer madness until just now."

"What do you mean?" I asked him.

"Sherlock's idea that the Black Friar could actually be . . . Mary Smeaton!"

I stopped to think. "Right . . . the daughter who avenges her betrayed father," I said thoughtfully.

But there was still another unanswered question.

"But Lupin," I said, "where do the coordinates in Sherlock's listing lead us?"

"To the Shad Thames tea and spice warehouses," Lupin replied. "And the direction 'early in the morning' should tell the Black Friar we'll be waiting there at dawn."

"Does that mean you're setting a trap for a killer?" I asked.

"Right again, Irene. How about you? Will you come with us?" he asked.

At dawn? At the Shad Thames tea warehouses? How would I be able to do it? I asked myself, without giving him an answer.

"I gave you the information," Lupin said as we left the building. "You'll think of how to get there, I'm sure."

He bent down to give me a peck on the cheek, but then, at the very last minute, turned and kissed me on the lips.

I turned beet red. "Hey!" I exclaimed, surprised. "How rude!"

"Pardon me, Miss Adler!" He laughed, pulling his hat over his eyes. Then he walked off down the sidewalk at full speed.

★ ★ ★

I went into my house feeling a little afraid. I had a clear sense that our friend Sherlock was in serious danger.

And with his stupid prank just now, Lupin had kissed me again. While the first time could have been a moment of confusion, this time was different. Could he have been waiting at the entrance to Miss Langtry's building, where he was sure no one would see us, with the ad in the *Times* just an excuse to be there? Or was I always making things complicated, and Lupin had just wanted to kid around?

At the same time, I couldn't help but think of Sherlock's hug from the night before, the reason for which, once again, escaped me.

Perhaps, I thought, *I should speak with them about it, as I don't want these simple misunderstandings to create a rift in our friendship.*

But I couldn't decide if that would be a good idea or not. *Should I speak to each of them separately, or should I discuss it when all three of us are together? What if it embarrassed them or perhaps set them against each other . . . and for what? For me?*

Once in my room, I gazed in my mirror, deep in thought as I tried to clarify things for myself. But all I saw was an impish smile on my face.

Sherlock or Arsène?

That was the question that caused me to smile — that and the glee I felt knowing that it was a question I couldn't answer. I was very comfortable with both of them, of course. But during the past few months with Sherlock, I had missed Arsène. Actually, we'd both missed him. In all our adventures, it had always been the three of us, but daily life was different.

"What a mess," I whispered, exhausted. And I wasn't just referring to the question of Sherlock or

Arsène. There was also the mess of the meeting at dawn that loomed ahead of us.

How would I get there? I wondered.

I bit my lip and nervously rearranged the silver combs on my dresser.

I realized that there was only one way I could get to the meeting — the same way that would hopefully clear things up with Sherlock and Lupin — and that was to be honest.

So before getting ready for bed, I looked for Mr. Nelson. I found him clearing the dinner table, and I told him everything honestly and without any hesitation.

After being reprimanded by my father for the incident in Notting Hill, Mr. Nelson no longer accompanied me in the carriage and mostly stayed home, as if he were being punished.

"At dawn where, Miss Irene?" he asked me, raising an eyebrow.

I repeated it, forcing myself to look him in the eyes, "The Shad Thames tea warehouses. I need you to come with me this time. It could be really dangerous."

"Really?" the butler asked.

I nodded.

He put down a plate he was carrying and said in a quiet voice, "Forgive me, but what makes you think I would be available to accompany you to such a dangerous meeting?"

"Because of what you told my father, right?" I smiled, a little bit embarrassed. "For my safety."

Since Mr. Nelson didn't respond, I took a deep breath and continued, "It was you, Mr. Nelson, who asked me to be honest with you. And I am being honest now. I need your help and possibly even your protection."

Mr. Nelson was puzzled, to say the least. "And what makes you think I won't immediately go tell your mother about this, to keep you from making another foolish mistake?" he asked.

"Because of what you told me last week," I replied. "That you're not a tattletale."

"Miss Adler . . . "

"I'd like you to go back to being my accomplice sometimes . . . not just a butler," I said.

Mr. Nelson nodded seriously, considering my offer.

"Is that a yes?" I asked him.

He stared at me. "Don't even think about it, Miss Irene. Furthermore, I suggest you go to your room right away."

Since I had thought for a moment that I might have been successful, my disappointment was even more bitter.

I went upstairs to get ready for bed and quickly said goodnight to my mother, who tried vainly to get me to leaf through some fashion magazines she had spread out on her bed like the tail of a peacock, and withdrew to my room.

"Oh, daughter, you're really a hopeless case!" I heard her scold me, though tenderly. "I know it doesn't matter much to you, but at least try to change your clothes more than once a week!"

She's right about that, I thought as I got ready for bed. I took off the jacket I'd worn for who knows how many days, hung it over the chair in front of the little mirror I had in my room, and checked my pockets for change. I was greatly surprised when I discovered a gold pendant in the shape of a heart in one of the outer pockets.

My expression in the mirror was now even more confused than before.

Who put it there? I wondered for almost the entire night. *Sherlock Holmes, when he hugged me after walking me home, or Arsène Lupin, when he kissed me by Miss Langtry's front door?*

Chapter 18

DAWN ON THE THAMES

I awoke sluggishly when I heard a faint knocking. It felt like I'd just fallen asleep. I slipped out from under the covers, thinking it might be one of Lupin's acrobatic visits, and felt the cold night air sting my skin. This time, though, the noise came from the door to my room. I opened it and found myself face to face with Horatio Nelson, who handed me a fur-lined coat. "It's very cold right before dawn, miss," he whispered. "Get ready quickly, or you'll be late!"

My heart leaped, and I hugged both the coat and Mr. Nelson in one fell swoop.

"Thank you, Mr. Nelson!" I said. "Thank you!"

"Shhh! Don't make so much noise or we'll be caught!" he whispered anxiously. "One hour — no more. Promise me?"

"I promise!" I whispered.

I went back in my room and put on the first clothes I laid my hands on. I carried my boots, so as not to make noise, and only put them on when I was at the front door.

Papa was traveling, and Mama was asleep. If we did everything carefully, she wouldn't awaken before we returned.

Mr. Nelson was wearing a dark, bell-shaped cape, which made him look daunting. Before leaving, he pulled his hat over his forehead and urged me to do likewise as he held the door open for me.

"How shall we go?" I asked him, as he closed the door with unexpected gracefulness.

"A carriage is waiting for us a block away," he responded. "To avoid making too much noise."

We walked to it swiftly, through a silent, white London, a stone maze spotted with piles of snow. We climbed into the carriage, and Mr. Nelson gave me his final instructions as we departed. "I'll have the carriage stop right after London Bridge widens," he said, "and I'll take you to the warehouses. Once we're there, we'll split up. Be aware, Miss Irene, there's an outdoor passageway that leads down to the Thames and separates the two main buildings. In this passageway, there are dozens of suspended footbridges. I'll watch over you from one of the highest ones, so that no one spots me, while you and your friends have your meeting."

"Thank you," I murmured. It reassured me to know that Mr. Nelson would be there.

Mr. Nelson placed his hand on his hip, and I saw a flash of something metallic. I looked more closely. Attached to his belt was a long dagger with a shiny handle in an ivory-inlaid sheath.

Then Mr. Nelson checked the time on a large pocket watch and leaned back against the seat, as if what we were about to do was normal.

★ ★ ★

We passed through a London that was slowly waking up. Some shopkeepers were opening up, and the first carts loaded with goods began to arrive from the countryside. On London Bridge, usually crowded with thousands of people, we only encountered a pair of carriages.

We got out of our carriage at a muddy hill covered with dirty snow, which sloped down to the bank of the Thames. The butler pointed to a five-story brick building with a dour façade and large doorways. We went in, walking down a long passageway.

Once inside, we found ourselves in a maze of empty rooms, but we heard distant footsteps echoing. Pungent smells wafted through the air. It seemed as if the walls were infused with the bitter aroma of tea, nutmeg, and other spices. I remember climbing up and down several flights of stairs, Mr. Nelson keeping a hand on my shoulder to guide me. Finally, he pointed to a door that led outside and motioned to go in that direction. He gestured to let me know that he would climb some stairs along the side of the warehouse and would soon be positioned above me.

"Just give me a few minutes, miss . . . and then go," he said.

"All right," I replied, nodding.

I waited as Mr. Nelson had requested. Then I left. I found myself on a metal footbridge extending between two buildings no more than a hundred feet from one another. Above and below me were about a dozen more walkways connecting the warehouses at different heights. On one side was the street, two floors below me. On the other side, the road went down to the loading area, along which lapped the cold waters of the Thames. It was a ghostly area, and slow tongues of fog crept up from the ground.

I immediately recognized Sherlock Holmes's rumpled coat on the footbridge below me and, a few footbridges over, Lupin's elegant brown one. Each of us was at a different height, on a different footbridge in this strange forest of metal.

We waved to each other and stayed where we were, waiting for someone else to come into view. In a few hours, dozens of porters and sailors would invade these empty rooms to transfer the sacks of spices from one warehouse to another, and from there, onto carriages and straight to grocery stores in the city. But at the moment, it was silent, hazy, and freezing.

I glanced at one of the footbridges above me, trying to locate Mr. Nelson. But my butler had vanished like a ghost.

"Someone's coming," Lupin said, pointing to a small door in the building in front of us. "Can you hear them?"

His voice, like our footsteps, echoed. I squinted, trying to identify which footbridge the person was approaching on. The echo made it hard to know with any certainty.

Then, in the middle of the footbridge between Sherlock and Lupin, on the side opposite us, a frail figure appeared, hobbling along and leaning on an elegant cane.

"It's not a woman," I whispered to Sherlock, leaning over the railing. I'd been expecting Mary and was disappointed it wasn't her. Perhaps it was a simple beggar who was hoping to find something in the empty warehouses.

"We're not only expecting a woman," Sherlock replied, smiling up at me.

"So who is it then?" I asked.

"You really don't know?" Sherlock whispered, as the other person, hunched over and wearing a hood, looked around, leaning on the railing of the bridge.

Sherlock pulled his coat around him and cleared his throat. "You remember that Smeaton's wife died giving birth to their second child? Look how the man walks. He's crippled, which happens to babies who are delivered by a doctor who isn't skilled."

I stared at the new arrival. "So that man is . . . Mary's brother?" I asked.

Sherlock raised his hand in greeting to the man, who had stopped on the footbridge. "Would you be the White Friar?" the man asked in a hoarse, irritated voice.

"I am, but my actual name is Holmes," my friend responded. "Sherlock Holmes. I'm pleased to meet the Black Friar. Or perhaps I should say . . . Adam Smeaton."

The man swayed on his good leg, grabbing the railing, and said, "What do you want from me?"

"I want you to confess to murdering Samuel Peccary and Joseph Barrow. And also confess that you intended to kill William Hallett."

The Black Friar raised his fist, furious. "You must be mad!"

"Really? Then it's a coincidence that the two ex-members of the Scarlet Rose Gang died at Twickenham and Wimpole Streets, as you specified in your chess problem?" Sherlock asked.

Adam grunted. "How did you crack the code?"

Sherlock laughed. "Did you really think it was a code? It was little more than child's play!"

"It wasn't meant for you!" Smeaton yelled.

"In fact, that's something I still don't understand: why did you publish it in the *Times*? Did you want to warn your father's former partners that you were coming to punish them?" Sherlock asked.

"You really don't know what you're talking about," Adam Smeaton snapped.

"Then why did you come to this meeting?" Lupin then intervened from his footbridge, just underneath the one on which Adam stood.

The man wasn't sure how to respond. "I thought it might be someone from the old gang. But I was wrong . . . you're just little boys," he said.

"Someone from the old gang . . . like Hallett, perhaps?" Sherlock asked. "Who apparently caught on and called on his guards to protect him?"

"We'll get him sooner or later," Adam spat.

"And how do you plan to do that with legs like yours?" Lupin asked him.

"Watch what you say!" Smeaton roared. "Keep mocking me, you two. No one will ever believe you."

He started to turn his back to leave, and it seemed that for him, this meeting was over.

"Not so fast, Adam!" With an aerialist's leap, Lupin jumped down to Smeaton's footbridge, and grabbing the railing, he dragged himself onto it like a cat. In the time it took the man to take two steps toward the warehouses — and before he could slide his hand under his coat — Lupin was beside him, blocking his arm.

I covered my mouth with my hand, terrified. Although Lupin was exceptionally athletic, he was still just a boy, while Adam, though he was frail, was a man.

"Leave me be!" Adam shouted, trying to wriggle away. As he did so, his hood slipped, showing his face. He had the face of a rodent, with tiny, darting eyes and a big nose scarred by scarlet fever.

"Not until you come with us to Scotland Yard!" Lupin shouted.

Adam pulled away again, which almost made him fall off the footbridge. We heard the ring of his iron cane as it fell. At that moment, a second voice echoed in the darkness between the warehouses.

"Nobody move," came a commanding female

voice. A woman appeared in front of me, on my own footbridge. She was tall, with a long, checkered coat, blond hair cut just above her shoulders, and a gun in her hand. She pointed it at me, then at Sherlock and Lupin, and then back at me, since I was only a few steps away from her. Sherlock slowly raised his hands in the air and murmured, "Don't do anything foolish, Mary."

It was her, Mary Smeaton!

"Nobody move!" the woman repeated, striking the metal floor with her heels as she paced. She gestured upward with the gun. "You, over there — I see you. Come out right now, hands in the air!"

I turned, thinking Mary had noticed Mr. Nelson, but instead saw Inspector Field step onto the footbridge above mine, his hands held high. "You're making a big mistake," he said.

"Throw your gun away! Now! Into the river!" Mary yelled.

After a moment, Field did as the woman ordered. Mary Smeaton walked right by me, and it was then that I saw her face. I recognized those icy eyes. They had the same gleam I saw for a brief moment in Ladbroke Square before I collapsed. The woman's face was marked by the strain of a hard life, and she looked many years older than she actually was. She had sunken eyes and deep wrinkles that dug grooves in her forehead, like stubborn scars. Her body looked portly and showed the effects of a poor diet.

"See that you stand here nicely, little girl . . . or yours will be the first pretty face I blow off. Got it?!" she shouted. She took my arm and twisted it behind my back, then pointed the gun under my chin. "Now listen carefully! I'm not sure what three brats like you are doing here, but I do know Inspector Field is famous for his young, poorly paid collaborators."

"That's nonsense!" Inspector Field blurted out.

Quick as a flash, Mary turned and shot him.

I remember the echo of that shot to this day, the first in my life I'd heard so close. And the most horrifying. The former agent to the Crown arched backward, swayed against the iron railing, and slid to the ground, grabbing his shoulder.

"You're mad!" he snarled in pain.

Mary Smeaton laughed evilly and continued to point her pistol at Sherlock and Lupin, moving it back and forth between the two. She ended by pointing the barrel — still warm — against my neck.

"It's a really nasty business for you three," she said. "A nasty business you shouldn't have stuck your noses into!"

I sensed an uncontrollable rage growing inside her that almost made the hand she was holding me with tremble. Yet I was so terrified, I could do absolutely nothing.

"But look at you!" the woman continued. "You could have stayed in the best schools in the country and in the warmth of your fancy bedrooms, and instead you landed in this nasty affair! In the most wicked neigborhood in this most wicked city! Go on, Adam! Get out of here! And you, dandy, stand up!"

"Are you talking to me?" Lupin said as Adam hobbled off the footbridge.

"Quiet!" Mary tossed her gun between her hands and then let off a second shot. It only missed Lupin because she had to aim high to avoid hitting Adam.

I saw Lupin turn white, lift his hands, and freeze, like a statue made of plaster.

My heart stopped. If I'd ever had any doubt, it was now clear that this was no longer just an adventure. Our lives were truly at risk.

"Come on!" Mary snarled. "I didn't wait twenty

years to be stopped by three brats and an old man. I certainly didn't wait twenty years for this! You!" she ordered Sherlock. "Hands behind your head and get next to the railing. This way, come on! Climb up! And then jump!"

Sherlock put his hands on the railing, but when he heard the order for him to jump down from a height of least twenty feet, he froze. "Ma'am —" he blurted out, turning to look at her.

"It's your choice," she said. "I can shoot you, or you can jump! If you're lucky, you'll break a leg or maybe both of them! But if I shoot you, you're too close for me to miss my target."

I tried to move, but her grip was as strong as a mastiff's bite.

"You, too!" she screamed at Lupin. "Step up to the railing!"

Unlike Sherlock, Arsène didn't make her say it twice. Swearing unrepeatable curses, he climbed up onto the railing and jumped into the void.

"NO!" I screamed.

I heard the thud of Lupin's body as it fell to the ground like dead weight. Then I heard him howl in pain, "My leg! My leg! Oh, my leg!"

It was a nightmarish situation, and there was no clear way of escaping. I tried to get free again, but Mary pushed me into the railing, knocking the wind out of my lungs. Then she whispered in my ear, "Your turn's next, little beauty, never fear. But you're lucky, because the river reaches this side."

Forced by the grip of her hand on my hair, I saw, thirty feet below me, the still, icy water of the Thames. It looked like a coffin.

"Now do you understand what it means to play with death?" Mary roared. She pushed me to the ground and pointed her gun at Sherlock, who was still frozen. Down on the ground, Lupin continued to roll around and scream horribly.

"Do you want this bullet or not — waaaaahhhhh!" Mary's words turned into a desperate wail. The young woman collapsed next to me. She lost her grip on the gun, which fell below.

There was a dagger sticking out of her shoulder.

Just then came the voice of Horatio Nelson. "Run, Miss Irene! Now!"

I turned and saw him above, ready to leap between the bridges. He must have taken advantage of the single moment that the killer had distanced herself from me to throw the dagger. And that throw had been brutally accurate.

The rest happened quickly. Sherlock disappeared inside the warehouses, and in the alley below me, Lupin stopped pretending to have broken his leg.

"I knew it!" I exclaimed to myself. He'd been too ready to jump, doing so only because his father had undoubtedly taught him how to fall without getting badly hurt. Indeed, that twenty-foot drop had apparently been little more than a hop for him.

I saw Lupin run to the gun that had fallen from Mary Smeaton's hand. And once again, I thought about what an amazing person my friend was.

"Look out!" Inspector Field shouted at me, his voice filled with pain.

In her own way, Mary was an extraordinary person, too. She had just pulled the dagger out of her shoulder and was holding it in her hand with a look that was at once terrible and terrified.

I shrank back, crawling on my hands and knees, but she didn't seem to see me. She dropped the dagger, turned, and ran.

My body was so full of excitement and adrenaline that all I thought to do was get up . . . and follow her.

"Miss Irene!" screamed Mr. Nelson, trying to make me see reason.

But I didn't listen. I ran across the echoing footbridge to the empty warehouse on the other side, passing through a room and running to the stairs following the sound of Mary Smeaton's heels. As we reached the street, I saw her and followed her at a distance. I heard many different sounds behind me, but they were like a fog I paid no attention to. I was fast, and she was wounded. I gained ground on her very quickly.

But what was I doing? And what would I do if I reached her?

Mary turned to check the distance between us, then did so again a few seconds later. It was then that I saw her finally grow alarmed. The mud, slush, and snow splashed beneath our boots.

When Mary realized I would reach her, she stopped, turned, and confronted me.

"You don't even know . . ." she panted ". . . what trouble . . . you've gotten yourself into . . . " She raised the hand she'd used to pull out the dagger, still filthy with blood. "I killed two men in cold blood . . . two cowards . . . and I will never be sure . . ."

"Quiet!" I screamed, having by now decided to hurl myself toward her.

Mary threw me one last look with those cold, sad eyes of her. She was very pale, and her sleeve was smeared with blood. I had taken my first step toward her when I saw her fall to the ground.

Without knowing why, I didn't stop rushing and went to kneel next to her in the mud. Was I afraid that, cunning as she was, she might be creating a scene so she could escape? Or perhaps I'd discovered it was possible to feel pity for someone, even if they had committed horrible deeds?

I only know that right then, my heart was a jumble of strong emotions I couldn't untangle.

When I realized that Mary was unconscious, I slowly stood up. My clothes were filthy. My hair had fallen around my face, and my hands were smeared with snow, mud, and who knows what else. I looked at Mary Smeaton's body, which was lying limp on the ground. She was breathing faintly . . . very faintly.

Mr. Nelson ran to me, out of breath. "Miss Irene! Are you —"

"I'm just a bit dirty, Mr. Nelson. Just a bit dirty," I interrupted abruptly.

Chapter 19

THE SHADOW OF VENGEANCE

While I was chasing Mary Smeaton, Lupin had seized Adam Smeaton and forced him to back down, gun in hand, while Sherlock had verified that Inspector Field's wound was not serious and helped him into a carriage (followed by the two Smeatons) to get him treated by a doctor.

Mr. Nelson and I returned home before Mama awoke. I couldn't let her see the condition of my clothing. I took a very long, hot bath. It only partly dissolved my tension, which lasted for so long that the following week's events are jumbled in my mind to this day, and even my diary can't help me sort them out.

Following the events at the Shad Thames warehouses, Inspector Field delivered the Smeaton siblings to Scotland Yard. He provided the officers with all the information needed to solve the Peccary and Barrow cases, along with evidence of the Smeaton siblings' connection to the Scarlet Rose Gang.

Before that took place, however, Sherlock, Lupin, and Inspector Field surveyed a certain apartment on Blackfriars Lane. Blackfriars Lane was where Adam Smeaton lived, and the name of the street explained the pseudonym he'd chosen for his fake chess problem.

Adam hadn't kept a proper diary. Through the years, though, he had papered his home with sheets of notes that according to Lupin, had created layers upon layers of wallpaper. They were attached to the walls, one on top of another, layered with glue.

Lupin read me a few passages, which only confirmed for me that Adam Smeaton was indeed insane.

As I listened, every single word caused the sound of the shot that had wounded Inspector Field to boom in my ears and reminded me of Mary's pained face, her wild eyes, and the desperate cry she'd let out when Mr. Nelson's dagger hit her.

The story of these crimes and the motivation behind them frightened me. They were the results of vengeance — an obsession that had lasted for over twenty years, ever since Mary and Adam's father had been betrayed.

As we'd guessed, the arrest of Gerald Smeaton, the leader of the Scarlet Rose Gang, took place because his accomplices ratted him out. When the police found him at his home, they wounded him with a bullet. Gerald didn't die immediately, though. He fled, and his body was only found several days later.

During those days he was missing, Gerald had instructed his two children to avenge him, making them swear they would do so. And so Mary and Adam made their father's last wish the great task of their lives. Their only goal.

"I am certain of only one thing," Adam wrote on one of the many pages filled with his raving notes and sketches. "And that is that Papa's three accomplices are like me — children of the grimy alleys of London's worst neigborhoods. I know they never left our city. They grew rich, yes, but London is the only place they understand and perhaps the only place that can understand them."

And he was right.

The young Adam had found work at the city's Land Registry Office. There, he combed through thousands of documents, day after day, month after month, year after year, searching for evidence of the three traitors. He had stayed at work long after closing, working feverishly by candlelight to avoid being discovered.

With meticulous madness, Adam had finally managed to find traces of each of his father's old partners. He'd reconstructed their name changes, relocations, sales, and real estate purchases. He'd figured out Peccary's new name and the location of his new home by tracking a jewel that had been given in payment for purchasing a plot of land.

As for Barrow, Adam had counted on the man's habit of painting the chimneys red on every house he lived in. Adam knew Hallett had a weakness for cemeteries, and it turned out that his house looked right onto the cemetery of a small church.

These were some of the details and clues that had allowed Adam to track down all three of his father's traitors.

Peccary, Barrow, and Hallett, who, along with Smeaton, had made up Scarlet Rose Gang, had been able to bury their infamous pasts by displaying their wealth and respectable associations. But they hadn't taken into account the intuitive mind and determined will of Adam Smeaton. Only Hallett had made the connection between the two homicides when he read about them in the papers, and he shut himself up in his home.

When Scotland Yard finally came knocking at his door, accusing him of crimes committed by the Scarlet Rose Gang twenty years before, Hallett was making plans for a quick getaway abroad. This plan would be thwarted, however, and he ended up spending a good number of years in prison.

Chapter 20

CHRISTMAS WITH FRIENDS

My memories of those days amaze and confuse me, even now. That particular day had begun so horribly and yet it was . . . Christmas Eve!

The hours passed quietly in the cozy atmosphere of our home. I was almost able to convince myself that what had taken place at the tea warehouses on the Thames was a bad dream. Our house was filled with the delicious aroma of a hearty broth, roasted chicken, smoked salmon from Scotland, and French goose liver paté (a product that could not be given up even in the midst of the Franco-Prussian War).

Papa was in an excellent mood and delivered news about the stormy political situation in Europe. But I listened more because I liked the sound of his voice than out of real interest in the conflict.

In the afternoon, I got ready to leave for the Shackleton Coffee House, bringing presents for Sherlock and Lupin with me. I heard my parents quietly whispering in the parlor, and I didn't interrupt them since I was sure they had important matters to discuss.

As I walked down the street, I thought about how the events of that morning had shaken me. But it was absolutely necessary to hide my state of mind from my parents. Luckily, the Christmasy atmosphere in the snowy streets helped me regain my typical good mood.

Those days, my life and spirit were much calmer than they would become later on. At that point, it would not be long before my true origins would be revealed to me. In fact, I received a clue about it that very day.

While I was walking between Mount and Davies Streets, a carriage came alongside me, and a woman's voice from inside asked me to stop. I obeyed, partly because I was lost in my thoughts and partly because the voice seemed pleasant and familiar.

I thought she wanted to ask for directions. But when the carriage came close, a gloved hand reached out the window and handed me an extremely elegant package. Just then, I heard a whisper from inside, "Merry Christmas, daughter."

I managed to distinguish the sparkle of two diamond rings and a woman's pale face. Her face seemed strangely familiar to me.

Then the carriage pulled away, leaving me on the curb with a Christmas present in my hands.

I opened it, letting the wrapping paper fall to the ground in my wonderment. It contained a delicate sketch: the profile, painted in white and pink, of a woman's face.

I held it against my chest, as if I knew her already.

As if I knew whom it depicted.

And then I started walking again.

★ ★ ★

The atmosphere at the Shackleton Coffee House was lively, and a fire roared in the hearth. The old wooden beams that held up the ceiling had been decorated with British flags and colorful streamers for the holidays.

I had to push my way through a crowd to get to our usual table with its worn-out armchairs. Inspector Field was there along with my two friends, his arm in a sling.

"Irene!" Lupin greeted me.

We all shook hands. Sherlock explained to me that the inspector had stopped by to wish us a merry Christmas and to fill us in on the latest details of the investigation.

"Did you finally sort out all your doubts?" I asked my friend, cheerfully and absently. I clasped the sketch between my fingers, wondering about the woman who had given it to me.

"Yes!" Sherlock exclaimed. "I finally understand why Adam Smeaton had to write that fake chess problem."

I sat down, pushing my gifts aside. "And what's that explanation?" I asked.

"Jealousy," Lupin answered, looking me in the eyes.

I was surprised. "What do you mean?"

"It would seem," Inspector Field said, appearing

to be enjoying himself greatly, "that Mary's husband not only forced her to marry him and had a violent temper, but that he was also tremendously jealous, to the point of reading all of his wife's correspondence."

"No!" I exclaimed.

"Just so," Sherlock continued. "It would seem that the two siblings had arranged a signal during one of Mary's rare visits to London to avoid Musgrave's jealousy. And so, when she saw the chess problem Adam had published, Mary left Liverpool and caught the first train to London to carry out the two murders."

"So she didn't lie to me," I whispered.

"She confessed to the police," Field explained. "It was she who killed both men, and she who robbed the two victims of personal objects as macabre trophies."

"It couldn't have been otherwise, considering her brother's frailty," Lupin said.

"He was the brains," Sherlock added, "and she was his arm."

"As well as his gun," I finished.

We laughed together, trading a few more jokes. Finally, I took out my two presents, which I gave to my dear friends, making sure they both noticed the heart-shaped pendant I wore around my neck.

However, I didn't detect any hint of recognition from either Sherlock or Lupin, and indeed, couldn't notice any difference between my two friends' expressions.

I had gotten them two identical copies of the book *A Christmas Carol* by Charles Dickens, the great writer who had recently died. Both told me they hadn't read it yet.

At that point, Inspector Field slapped his hands on his knees and announced he was leaving.

"May I ask you one last thing, Inspector?" Sherlock Holmes asked.

"Of course, young man. What can I do for you?" the man replied.

"What's the name of your young colleague," Sherlock asked, "the one who, like me, figured out the Black Friar's code?"

The inspector didn't seem to remember the person Sherlock was asking about, so I rushed to his aid. "Oh, yes, Inspector! That young man you said you'd introduce us to someday . . . nicknamed the Shadow?"

Only then did Inspector Field nod. With a huge smile, he announced, "Ah, yes. My young colleague is named James . . . James Moriarty. I really hope you can meet someday!"

METROPOLITAN
BURGHS AND   SOUTHERN

PLAN of LONDON

drawn and engraved by   J.B. LANAHAN

& EASTERN ENVIRONS

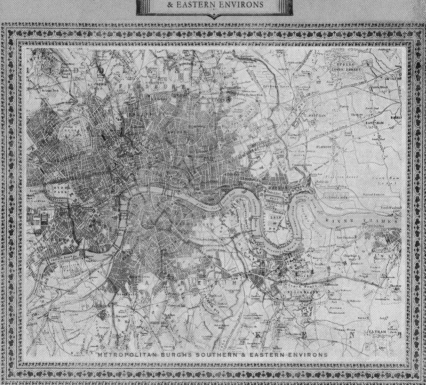

METROPOLITAN BURGHS SOUTHERN & EASTERN ENVIRONS